About the Author

T B Carlton is a writer currently residing in Norway, where she grew up. A lover of animals, she has spent time working with horses, enjoying nature all the while devouring books. She started writing at the age of six and it is a passion that has stayed with her throughout her whole life. She draws on a wide range of inspirations like the books of Astrid Lindgren, Tove Janson, as well as Lemony Snicket, Edgar Allan Poe and the works of Tim Burton. *Eliza Through the Portal* is her debut novel.

Eliza
Through the Portal

T.B. Carlton

Eliza
Through the Portal

Nightingale Books

NIGHTINGALE PAPERBACK

© Copyright 2024
T. B. Carlton

The right of T. B. Carlton to be identified as author of
this work has been asserted by them in accordance with the
Copyright, Designs and Patents Act 1988.

All Rights Reserved

No reproduction, copy or transmission of this publication
may be made without written permission.
No paragraph of this publication may be reproduced,
copied or transmitted save with the written permission of the
publisher, or in accordance with the provisions
of the Copyright Act 1956 (as amended).

Any person who commits any unauthorised act in relation to
this publication may be liable to criminal
prosecution and civil claims for damages.

A CIP catalogue record for this title is
available from the British Library.

ISBN 978 1 83875 593 5

*Nightingale Books is an imprint of
Pegasus Elliot Mackenzie Publishers Ltd.*
www.pegasuspublishers.com

This is a work of fiction. Names, characters, businesses, places, events and
incidents are either the product of the author's imagination or used in a
fictitious manner. Any resemblance to actual persons, living or dead, or
events is purely coincidental

First Published in 2024

**Nightingale Books
Sheraton House Castle Park
Cambridge England**

Printed & Bound in Great Britain

Dedication

To the child I used to be, the future will be brighter

Acknowledgements

Thanks Lars, for all our dog walks and brainstorms in the night.

Chapter 1
Late Night Ballet

It was a dreary October night, and a chill had set in. Eliza lay in the big bed, unable to sleep yet unwilling to move, for her grandparents did not take well to bumps in the night that might cause them to wake up. Eliza hadn't wanted to stay over with her grandparents. Oh, they were nice enough people like most grandparents are. They were heavy on the hugs yet low on patience, and a wild, stubborn and often loud eleven-year-old was not something they wanted to put up with for long durations. It was almost midnight, way beyond her bedtime of half past nine, but sleep had evaded her, as it often did at the old house her grandparents owned. She had been told it was quite the old house too, about two hundred years or more, and not much had changed in that time. The interior walls, beams and windows were as old as her grandparents, with blotches of paint falling off in some places. The dark wood stood out from under the white paint that had been used on almost all the surfaces in Eliza's bedroom. Every wooden panel in the floor creaked and the stairs leading up to the attic sounded like an entire orchestra of moaning trees if you so much as looked at it too hard. She was very curious about what was hidden up there, for surely such a staircase must guard something exciting. One does not place a hound before a door unless there are treasures behind it. However, the fear of awakening her grandparents kept her in bed.

So, in bed she lay, as still as a mouse. For about thirty minutes more. Then, as gentle as a snake, she slithered out of her bed. Her long white nightgown was still warm, and with her bunny slippers on, she made her way across the floor. A song came to her mind then. Earlier that evening her grandmother had shown her a ballet called *Swan Lake*. Eliza had started taking classes when she was six and felt quite the master already, so she had been excited to see the dances, the beautiful gowns and the funny music as her grandmother talked her through the show, for there was no talking in a ballet performance.

As she was thinking this, one of the dance numbers, *Dance of the Little Swans*, came into her head, as she stepped lightly across the floor. The routine played in her head step-stop, step-stop, dum-da, dum-da, dum-da dam-dam da-ra-da-ra-da, went the song. It didn't take her long to get to the door at the end of the room, and just as she reached for the door handle, she misstepped and heard a *creeaaking* sound. Eliza winced, stopped all movement and strained her ears. Hearing nothing, not even the faint snores of her grandfather, she crept on.

The hallway outside the bedroom was luckily empty. Eliza turned her head to the left where her grandparents' bedroom lay. Their door was shut and there were no lights coming from under the door. Heaving a sigh and closing her eyes Eliza missed the subtle move of the shadows to her right. She opened her eyes. She had a decision to make. Should she go down the creaky stairs to the kitchen where she knew a leftover piece of cake lay hidden away and barricade herself on the couch with some cake, milk and a grown up TV show? Or should she brave the night, and go exploring the old house and its many secrets? Eliza chewed her lip in contemplation. It was a wonderful night and she was wide awake. Turning on the TV would surely awaken her grandparents, and then there would be hell to pay. They took no prisoners when it came to punishment, and Eliza would rather end her visit on a good note. So, seeing no other choice (for going back to bed was not an option), she took a deep breath and steered towards her right and towards the stairs up to the attic.

Chapter 2
The Attic

Eliza had been told that attics were no place for children, no place to play or wander about in. So naturally, she was dying to explore them; had been since she was a little girl. However, since her parents' house only had a basement, and she would never go down there, there were not a lot of attics to explore except for the one at her grandparents' house. Yet she was met with a stern "NO!" when she had asked last year if she could venture up there. Now there was no one to stop her, and Eliza could barely contain her excitement.

Steering towards the rickety old staircase, walking on the tips of her toes as quietly and quickly as she could, Eliza's mind raced with wonder, thinking of all the treasures that could be hidden away up there.

Maybe there's a big chest filled with pirate treasure! Gold coins, big crowns and shiny emeralds that she could adorn her clothes with, making the other girls in her class green with envy, for they would surely not have anything akin to those, Eliza thought, smiling from ear to ear.

Or, her smile faltered, the attic might be a hiding place for monsters! Big, green, slimy creatures, with six eyes and pointy teeth. Tiny, purple, horned beasts who climbed up your legs and gnawed on your arms! She stopped, one foot almost at the first step on the staircase. What would she do if there were monsters up there? Maybe that was why she had been told to stay away — To keep her away from the monsters, or to keep the monsters away from her? No, she couldn't think like that, and either way she had to find out for herself. She wasn't afraid of the monsters. No, they should be afraid of her! She would find a sword and fight them, fight them all until the very end, and she would be known as 'monster slayer Eliza Roberts', the girl who dared to fight! With new confidence, Eliza started to walk carefully up the stairs.

They were as old as the house, crooked in most places, worn out in others with dark brown paint giving way for the wood's natural colour underneath. Too focused on not making a sound, eyes staying on the steps of the stairs, she didn't notice the shadows moving on the top of the stairs and the halting of their movements as they noticed the girl. Had Eliza looked up then and strained her eyes to see to the top of the stairs, she would have seen them. Her next step landed a bit too hard and a groaning creak sounded in the seemingly empty hallway. Eliza froze, certain that she would be discovered this time. She almost stopped breathing, strained her ears and waited. Five seconds, ten, then twenty seconds later and no sign of an angry grandparent. Eliza sighed and was about to continue up the final two steps when a "clank!" of what sounded like glass landing on a carpet sounded from above her, from inside the attic.

She should run. She should run back down to her grandparents, jump into their bed and hide until the morning. She should wake them up and tell them there was someone or something in the attic and they needed to get rid of it! Eliza should have done that, but she was frozen to the spot, unwilling or unable to move anywhere. About to call out, she thought better of it. If there were people, monsters or worse hiding in the attic, calling attention to herself was the last thing she needed, for she had read enough detective books with her grandmother to know that one had to have the element of surprise when sneaking up on someone. Eliza had decided…

She would have to investigate the strange noise herself. Her breath came out in short puffs of air, still breathing quickly from the scare, and she fought to calm her breathing, for she knew what she had to do, and she needed all the bravery she could muster to even dare to enter the attic. Taking the last steps in one big move, she stood outside the old door.

This time when she listened, Eliza swore she heard voices gently talking from behind it, and was that a faint melody? More curious than ever, she forgot herself, her foot landing hard on the old hardwood floor and the resounding *creaaak* that followed made her gasp before clasping her hands together over her face. But too late, she found out, for when she removed her hand she found that the big door to the attic had opened, and the darkness that lay before her was not like any darkness she had seen before. It enveloped the spacious room yet didn't reach the floor outside where she stood, nor the stairs behind her. Braving one step, Eliza held her breath as she entered the room before letting it slowly out in astonishment, for nothing in her head had prepared her for what she now saw.

Chapter 3
"Tea, dear?"

The attic was boring. Some big furniture draped in old sheets, some suitcases from the last century, and a gramophone standing near one wall that took up most of the spacious room, apart from an open space in the middle of the room, but no pirate treasures, no place to hide monsters, be they big or small; and finally, she saw no one. Eliza walked slowly the rest of the way into the attic and turned around several times, trying desperately to find the source of the noises she had overheard. Finding nothing you wouldn't have expected from any other normal attic, she started to look closer behind, under and over the furniture.

They must be hiding! She thought, as the only thing out of the ordinary was an old, tattered, blue-chequered tablecloth on the ground under the only window in the room, and on it was a peculiar child's tea set placed there as if someone were in the middle of their afternoon tea. She looked high and low, yet found no one, not even a mouse's droppings. Heaving a sigh, Eliza shook her head and then stamped her foot in anger, for she had been so brave and had hoped to get to the bottom of the mystery.

"Stomping yer foot like that'll only make a hole in the ground, young lady!" an old voice croaked from behind her.

Eliza spun around, eyes big as apples as they searched for the owner of the voice.

"Who's there?" Eliza whispered before clearing her throat. "Come out this instant! It's not polite to hide." Eliza yelled. Her voice was stronger, showing an anger that she did not feel, but she felt she needed to sound more grown up, it usually helped to make people take her more seriously.

A mist had started to grow around the shiny brown wardrobe at the end of the room from Eliza now. No, not a mist exactly, but a grey, bleary cloud that, as she stared at it, took on more and more shape until there, standing, or floating before her were three shapes that looked to be human. On the left side there were what looked to be a man, younger than her grandfather yet older than her father, dressed strangely in a dusty top hat sitting slightly crooked on his head, a dress coat slightly too big on his frame and what looked to have once been nice trousers, just like the ones her father wore to work.

Eliza noted that he had no shoes, or more precisely, he had no feet! not any that she could see anyway. His face gave away his age, with lines going in all directions and hairs sticking out of his ears, yet with big eyes that held a youthful glimmer of mischief. The other two looked to be women. One somewhat older but neither were young; both wearing puffy dresses with high collars and pretty embroidery on the skirts, but where one's hair was light, probably blonde and rolled high up on her head, the other's was loose in a mess of dark, thick curls around her face. The latter seemed also to be the youngest.

"Gerald, Dear, you scared the poor child!" The older of the two women said as she looked sternly at the man before looking back at Eliza.

"I hope Gerald didn't frighten you too badly, child. My name is Victoria, this gentleman is my late husband Gerald, and this lady here is my dearest friend Anne."

The woman with the dark curls smiled gently at Eliza as the man, Gerald, took off his hat in greeting, before looking back at Victoria sheepishly.

"Yes, sorry about that. Didn't mean to frighten ya too badly!"

His accent was different from that of the other two. Eliza was still standing frozen to the ground unwilling to look away from the people — if she could call them that — who had spoken to her. She couldn't believe her eyes and kept looking from one person to the next without stopping, not knowing what to say. Noticing that her mouth was hanging open, Eliza shut it with a snap. As the seconds ticked by and the three people kept floating in front of her, looking at her expectantly, Eliza tried to find a question to ask, like 'who are you?' or

'What are you doing in my grandparents attic?' Instead she simply asked, "W-what are you?"

Not waiting for a reply, she jumped back and put her arms up. At school she had learnt from some of the boys that if you met someone you didn't know, and you had no grownups with you, intimidation was the best way to keep yourself from harm. Eliza's face was set hard in a frown although her arms were trembling. 'Could one fight these things? Would she be strong enough to do so'? She didn't care.

"I'm not afraid of you!" It was only a little lie, for as curious as these people were, and as badly as she didn't want to fight, the hair on the back of her neck stood up as the figure before her spoke.

"There will be no need for a quarrel, so put your hands down, young lady!" The older of the women said sternly and glided closer to Eliza. "We mean you no harm. We are, as I believe you call them, ghosts. Long ago, before you were born, we lived in this house for many years. We had tea, went to work and socialised with guests, just like you do."

The older woman, Victoria her name was, smiled gently at Eliza, but the smile did not reach her eyes, for as cloudy as they seemed at first, they were hard, as if they were rocks. Eliza got the feeling that they would be able to see right through her if given the chance. Slowly lowering her hands, Eliza thought about what the woman had said. 'If they really were ghosts, why could she see them'?

"Why can I see you?" she finally asked.

The ghosts looked at each other in turn before the younger of the two women lowered herself into one of the chairs closest to Eliza.

"We're not really sure, no one has ever seen us before. However, we have not met a child since we've been here!"

The answer was good enough for Eliza, who grew more and more curious, and less afraid by the minute. She took a step closer to the ghosts, her bare feet touching the end of the tablecloth on the ground. She looked down on it and cocked her head to the side.

"Were you having a tea party?"

At this, the ghosts that were still in the air, floated to the ground near the other end of the tablecloth where their teacups stood. Gerald picked his cup up and took a sip of what Eliza had assumed was an empty cup, for it now seemed to be filled with a light brown liquid. Not wanting to be impolite, she sat down as well, and as soon as she did, another cup was sat before her. Surprise clear in her face, Eliza picked it up. The cup was old, very old, that much was clear, it looked as if it was made of the finest porcelain with light blue painted flowers around the outside with a slight crack on the rim. It was empty. Victoria cleared her throat and as Eliza looked up at her, she saw the woman holding a matching teapot.

"Would you care to join us for tea, dear?" As she said this, Victoria held the teapot out towards Eliza.

Eliza suddenly felt unsure. She didn't know these people, and if her grandparents found out she was having tea with strangers in their attic, they would have a fit for sure! She turned her head towards the attic door, it was almost closed, 'when had that happened'? Yet she wanted to know more about these people, then they wouldn't be strangers, and no one could be mad at her for having tea with friends. A smile spread on her face as she turned back towards her hosts.

"I would be delighted to!" came her reply.

Chapter 4
News about the Outside

All three of the ghosts smiled at her, and Anne clapped her hands together before joining them around the tea set. Eliza's teacup was filled and so the conversations started.

"Who may you be, child?" Gerald asked between sips of tea.

"I'm Eliza, I'm here visiting my grandparents for the weekend!"

"Pleasure to make your acquaintance, Eliza. Now, would you please tell us of your world?" Victoria asked for they were anxious for news about the world outside.

They had not been out of the house for over a century, and as they had observed from the other rooms in the house, much had changed since their time. Although Gerald had died a few years before his beloved Victoria, and five years before Anne, what they knew, seen and lived was long since gone, and news reached them so rarely.

Eliza told them all that she could think of when it came to her world, although had the ghosts asked a grownup, they would have received some different answers. She told them of what she knew; about the cold weather, her favourite TV shows and how rarely she got to watch TV, as opposed to her friends back home. The TV, the ghost had seen TV progress from huge boulder size squares to the flat screens of the day.

She told them about the new car her father had bought that ran on electricity alone. After that, she had to tell them how a car looked on the inside, for Gerald had seen one from the window downstairs and had found the motor vehicle quite fascinating indeed! Then she told them about her friends, the games they played on the field behind their school. Victoria was shocked to say the least when she heard that boys and girls of all ages played football, together, without supervision by guardians. Her whole body shook, and Eliza thought she reminded her of one of the chickens she had seen, ruffling her feathers briskly. Anne had giggled at Victoria's expression and asked if Eliza enjoyed sports as well. She did, she was good at football too. As they talked, drank their tea and laughed, Eliza felt more and more safe amongst her newfound friends, so she thought it was time to ask some questions herself.

"Why are you here?" Eliza asked with a frankness only an 11-year-old could possess. "Are there others like you?"

"Why yes, yes I do believe there are. We have never met others, yet I would be surprised if we were the first and only ghosts to ever exist on earth!" Victoria replied with as much certainty as she could have, given.

"As for why we are, I cannot answer you my child, for we do not know."

Eliza had the feeling that there was something they weren't telling her, but she shrugged it off for now.

Taking a sip of her tea, enjoying the warmth it brought to her body and mind, Eliza thought of her next questions, for there were so many of them, and she didn't know how long she would have to ask them all. She wanted to know more about how they came to be here, for she knew that they would have had to die to become ghosts and she wondered if only humans could become ghosts or if animals could as well.

"My family had a dog, Billie, when I was younger, but he died almost a year ago, do you think he is a ghost too?"

Eliza didn't know what she wanted them to answer, really. She had loved that dog with all her heart, but her father had said that Billie had gone to doggy heaven, were he would run around and play all day with other dogs, and if he were a ghost, he must be somewhere alone, with no one to play with, and that made her sad when she thought about it.

The ghosts looked at each other, not knowing what to say or who should reply. Anne cleared her throat before looking at Eliza with warmth in her clear eyes that calmed the young girl.

"No, I don't think they can be, dear. When I was alive, I too lost my beloved companion, Bella, to an illness before her time. My grief was long and dark until one day my governess told me that Bella was somewhere safe and was healthy and strong; for there is a special place for the gentle creatures that we love, and there nothing can harm them, and they have all the company and love their hearts desire."

Eliza smiled at Anne before nodding her agreement, dark curls bobbing around her head as she moved a little closer to the ghost before answering.

"My father said something similar when Billie died, but I was still sad, knowing I wouldn't be able to hold him again, but I feel better now, knowing he is happy, playing with Bella and the others!"

Anne returned Eliza's smile with one of her own, moving the hand not holding her teacup through her dark curls before settling it in her lap. A few more questions, none big or important, filled the silence afterwards and Eliza felt herself relax more and more in the presence of the ghosts, her new friends, and all thoughts of her grandparents and their possible anger at finding her gone from her bed at night were gone.

That was until Gerald let out a groan and stretched, or so it seemed to Eliza; for his body, instead of standing -or floating- up, started to stretch upwards, although his lower body remained on the floor! He stretched and grew until his arms nearly hit the crooked ceiling above them, then his back gave an audible 'POP!'- sound, and he shrank back to the ground. Eliza had to almost lift her jaw from the floor, for she had never seen anything like that, she didn't even know people could do that.

Yet, a voice in her head said, *they are not people, not any more.*

Gerald took no notice of Eliza's surprised expression when he returned to his normal body length. Instead, he clapped his hands together and looked at the group of both the living and the dead, the mischievous glint back in his eyes.

"Now ladies, this was a most lovely tea party, I truly enjoyed it." Gerald bowed low to the ground before continuing.

"Would you lovely ladies care to join me in a dance?"

Chapter 5
The Midnight Dance

Anne looked overcome with joy. Her eyes sparkled with barely held excitement as she looked at Victoria and took the other woman's hand between her own.

"Dear Victoria, it has been so long since we danced, and it would bring me the utmost joy if you were to join as well!"

Anne knew that Victoria rarely danced, even when she had been alive. The older woman preferred staying in with her newest novel rather than join Anne and Gerald at a gathering or a cotillion. They never minded Victoria's refusals, wanting their friend to be content, and if that was with a book, in a cosy chair in the couple's library, then they would gladly let her stay; but that was years ago, and Anne wanted to dance. So, with her plea to the other woman, Anne hoped Victoria would want to dance. Victoria looked as if she was going to refuse and looked at her dear friend sternly.

"Oh, all right, I'll dance tonight, since we have a guest with us, and it would not be proper to reject your pleas, dear;" yet her lips pursed.

Eliza didn't know what was going on, were they going to dance? Here in the creaky, cramped attic? Wouldn't that make an awful amount of noise? It would surely wake her grandparents, and then she would have to leave her friends, and she wasn't ready for their encounter to be over just yet. Biting her lip and listening to Gerald happily explaining that he had just the right musical disc to play (whether this was an old record or a CD she didn't know). Anne rose and twirled around them.

Eliza asked her question. "Won't the noise wake my grandparents? I mean, I heard you when I was standing on the bottom of the stairs leading up here, and that was only a small sound. Wouldn't music be heard all around the house?"

Gerald was the one to answer her, now floating above the ground in his usual way, pulling out an old pocket watch as he did.

"Oh no, dear. The sounds we make mostly go unnoticed by the living, unless we want them to be heard, that is. We have had arguments, dances and moved the furniture about when we felt like it and have never been heard. That is, until you showed up tonight."

This seemed to puzzle the man, as if the notion of suddenly being heard without their knowledge was something he had never thought about, Eliza realised that it might well be so.

"Well then, what sort of dance are we dancing? I don't know a lot of different ones, and no old-timey ones for sure."

Anne gave a light laugh, Victoria harrumphed and Gerald moved towards the old gramophone Eliza had remembered seeing as she first entered the attic. She was a little taken aback by their reactions, seeing that it seemed to her to be a reasonable question. She didn't know many dances. She was eleven years old and besides her ballet, she hadn't had that much experience aside from just moving about to the music her parents or grandparents played. The ghosts probably knew hundreds or thousands of dances from when they were alive and songs long forgotten by the outside world. She crossed her arms, for she was still sitting and couldn't show her confusion and uncertainty another way, for she would not sulk. She wasn't seven any more.

"What? What is this you're not telling me?" Eliza couldn't, however, keep the anxiety out of her voice.

This sobered the ghosts, for they were at once close to her again, all with calming looks and knowing smiles.

What she didn't know, was that their dance was not a regular dance. Oh, the ghosts could dance any number of dances as Eliza had thought, ranging from a Polka to the Waltz. They did however have a special dance, a ghost dance one could only dance to when one was either dead, or accompanied by the departed. The ghosts didn't know where they had learnt it, they only knew that now was the time to dance it and dance it they would. Victoria placed a gentle hand on Eliza's shoulder, startling them both, for neither was certain the other could be touched before now. Regaining her composure first, Victoria gave the young girl a wink, before asking Gerald to turn on the music.

Then the strangest thing in Eliza's young life happened. A soft yet uplifting tune played from the gramophone. It ebbed and flowed through the air, making its inhabitants sway with it, string instruments lulling them along. Then Victoria rose taking Gerald's outstretched hand as he twirled her into his arms. Then they were off, twirling slowly around the attic as if it were a grand ballroom in a castle somewhere.

Eliza felt both giddy and a little insecure about the dance, then she felt a sudden thump coming from inside her chest as the music picked up its pace, her heart following the beat. She felt more when saw Anne's outstretched hand, and her insecurities fell away as her hand touched Anne's, a smile mirrored on all their faces. A drumbeat joined the strings and flutes in the song, as they all threw themselves across the attic floor, twirling and jumping along. Eliza felt ecstatic as Anne lifted her in an elaborate jump, then a twirl, before she suddenly found herself dancing with Gerald, his smile lighting up the entire room. No, not just his smile, for the room itself seemed brighter; the floor a white marble, the walls a deep red and as Eliza was lifted again above the ground, she saw that they were not in the old attic of her grandparents' house. They were not in an attic at all! The room was twice if not three times the size of the attic, and where there once was old furniture, there was open space, a live orchestra performing, and hanging from the no longer small and crooked ceiling -now as tall as a cathedral- was the largest chandelier Eliza had ever seen.

As she was again twirled by Gerald in their ever moving dance, Eliza cast a glance at the other ghosts and was astounded by what she saw. In full colour, heavy blues, deep greens, golden blonde and warm brown, Victoria and Anne danced.

'Oh how regal they look,' thought Eliza, and how she wished she looked like them. She couldn't think about it for too long, for the dance sped up, and Gerald, she now saw, in a well-tailored suit and unbroken top hat, brought her into the middle of the dance floor to meet the other women. Laughter mingled with the crescendos and bangs from the orchestra across the room as the dancers almost collided with each other, before they all joined hands, dancing in a ring, faster and faster. Eliza never knew she could dance so fast without falling, and she squealed with delight, closed her eyes and let herself go. She had no idea of how long they danced for, as she found herself becoming more and more hectic and less coordinated with each passing minute. As the song neared its end, Eliza felt Gerald stumble. As a domino stack, one after the other fell after him, Gerald first, then Eliza, followed by Victoria and Anne. Eliza was laughing so hard that she hadn't noticed that the music had stopped altogether, and as she opened her eyes, she found herself in a heap of arms, legs, hair and teacups, back in her grandparents' attic.

As her laughter subsided, Eliza looked around her, wanting to thank her friends for the dance and although she had more questions to ask, her friends were nowhere to be seen. She was alone. Then she heard the chime from the grandfather clock downstairs. Two, five, eight-twelve. It was midnight.

Chapter 6
What to do Now?

Her body heavy and her mind running a mile a minute Eliza got up and started walking towards the door leading out of the attic. Feeling very tired suddenly, as the evening finally hit her, Eliza walked down the stairs as gently as she could, crept into her bedroom and with a deep sigh she fell into her bed and was asleep as soon as her head hit her pillow.

Eliza woke to the sounds of tinkering from downstairs, most likely the kitchen. Her grandmother was known for rising early and making coffee first thing. Little by little, the night slowly trickled back into focus. The attic, the ghosts, the dance, oh what a dance it had been! Yet the more Eliza thought, the less real it seemed to have been. Had it been a dream? Surely not, for she remembered everything, she could still feel the touch from each of the ghosts as they had danced. Then again how could it be real? Ghosts in her grandparents' attic? She shook her head, feeling foolish. There was no such thing as ghosts, her father had told her so after she had a nightmare a few years ago, so naturally, the people from last night, her friends, were just a dream, or a figment of her imagination. She had been told it was quite lively.

Reassured that it had been a dream, Eliza scampered downstairs, ready for breakfast and a new day, for she had plans to explore the vast yard behind her grandparents' house. When she had visited before it had always been raining, or snowing, and she had been ordered not to go outside for fear of tracking in mud, snow or God knows what else.

Now luck was in her favour, for as she ran down the stairs to the kitchen, Eliza glimpsed blue skies and sunshine through a window just before the first steps down. She would eat, say hello to her grandparents, and then race outside before they could stop her, for the grounds that came with the house were large and unexplored.

Eliza came to an abrupt stop at the kitchen, for just then the lovely smell of pancakes hit her nose. Her grandmother's famous breakfast cakes were something to yearn for, with melted butter, chocolate chips and whipped cream. They were a feast for a young child, and just what Eliza needed for her exploring. Her grandmother, an old, slightly frumpy round woman, was one of the kindest old ladies Eliza knew. To be fair, she didn't know a lot of them, yet she reckoned none were as kind as her. Oh, grandmother had her limits; no eating in the living room, no running in the halls and most of all, no throwing of toys or balls inside, lest you break something and be sent to bed without supper.

Grandmother was standing by the stove, flipping a pancake as she hummed along to an old song on the radio, one she had probably listened to as a child. Her apron was a lilac frilly thing, with white embroidery around it and some stains that had been there for as long as Eliza could remember. She wore pink fluffy slippers and her hair was still in curlers, for no matter the day of the week, grandmother wanted to look her best. As if she had felt Eliza's stare, and without looking up from where she poured more batter into the pan, her grandmother called out to the girl.

"Good Morning my girl, what's the great rush this morning?"

Eliza felt a blush creeping up her neck.

"I'm fine thank you! Gon esplor the gardn latr…" Eliza swallowed the huge bite before continuing. "…and I wondered if I could borrow a pair of rain boots, as all I have are my new sneakers, and I promised mom not to get them dirty so early, and I have a lot of work to do!"

Her grandmother chuckled, trying to piece together exactly what her granddaughter had meant. Most likely the garden. 'She always wants to go out there,' she thought to herself.

"I do have an old pair in the closet in the hall, they're a bit big, but they'll just have to do!"

Having just put the last piece of food into her mouth, Eliza jumped up from her seat and ran over to hug her grandmother, her arms barely reaching halfway around the old woman.

"But before you run outside, go upstairs, wash and get dressed! You can't go outside in your nightgown." That was said while her grandmother shook her head, for she feared Eliza was likely to do exactly that and thanked the heavens that their nearest neighbour lived ten minutes, away in case Eliza didn't listen.

Eliza ran out of the kitchen and almost collided with her nearly awake grandfather, who spluttered and shouted after the girl to slow down. However, his pleas fell on deaf ears.

Already back in her bedroom, Eliza ran about as she got herself ready. Pulling her dark hair into a ponytail at the same time as she pulled on her socks turned out be harder than it seemed, for before she knew it, Eliza tipped forwards and hit the floor with a *thud.* Exasperated, she removed her nightgown and exchanged it for an oversized blue and white wool jumper with a large cat knitted on the front. Her faded, purple jeans followed. Throwing a glance in the mirror hanging above her dresser, Eliza wiped away the specks of chocolate from the sides of her mouth and looked into her hazel eyes, squinting like she usually did, before giving a nod. She was ready.

Taking two steps at a time and jumping over the remaining three last ones, Eliza hit the floor of the hallway. She walked over to the closet and tried to find the old boots. There were shoes of all sizes, colours, and functions, most had pairs, but some stood alone. Most just lay in a heap at the bottom. Then out of the corner of her eye, Eliza saw what must be the boots. A pair of slightly damaged, muddy dark red rainboots lay at the bottom of the pile. They must have been at least three sizes too large for her, but Eliza saw no problem there; they were perfect.

The grounds outside the house was frozen solid in the early morning. Though the light of the sun shone bright and warm, Eliza's breath puffed out like a cloud. She breathed deeply in and out a few times, pretending to be a great dragon, stomping around over the frozen hydrangeas in her grandmother's flower beds. A murder of crows startled up from a tree nearby in the otherwise quiet day. The sun reflecting on their dark bodies before they vanished behind the large patch of woods at the end of the yard. Jumping over the rocks and dead plants around her, Eliza wondered when was the last time anyone did anything out there. The only thing that looked to have seen some tenderness was her grandmother's flowers, now all dead from the frost, and the small patch of grass by the back door. What else she could see of the yard were weeds, small rocks and tree roots jutting up from the ground. The rest of the grounds were hidden within the woods she now entered, tall pine trees stretching up towards the sky and growing so thick in some places that the sun couldn't reach through.

Eliza crept her way inwards, keeping as quiet as she could, for her grandmother had told her that if one kept very gentle and calm, one could catch a glimpse of the wild rabbits that roamed the woods. With inquisitive eyes kept strained on the ground around her, Eliza didn't notice the large root sticking up from the ground right in her path before she stumbled over it, meeting the ground hard. She was about to let out a cry, for she had landed with her knee first and it had been scraped through her pants, and she could feel a bit of blood trickling down, when she saw it.

A large rabbit crouched low by a bush to her left. Its large ears pointed in different directions as it sniffed the ground before abruptly looking up, directly at her. Eliza held her breath in fear of scaring it away. She tried to stand up, at least to get her body up from the cold, wet ground. The rabbit continued to look at her, blinking quickly, twitching its nose, before it took off through the bush. Eliza got up and ran after it, snagging herself on the low branches of the trees around her, never losing sight of the rabbit. She ran for what seemed like forever, following the rabbit over bushes, ducking under branches and stumbling before she came to a clearing. The rabbit had stopped right in front of a little shed that stood in the middle of the clearing and now it turned towards her, as if to see if she had followed. Eliza walked slowly up to it, yet it didn't move, it waited until she was within arms' reach before setting itself on its rear legs and waited.

Unsure of what to do, and out of breath, she bent down and as gently as she could, picked the rabbit up and held it in front of her, looking into its eyes.

"You're not afraid of me, are you?" she asked the rabbit, breathing heavily. It blinked back at her, not giving any reply. "Why have you brought me here, silly rabbit? Do you want to show me something, this old shed perhaps?" Eliza brought the rabbit close and cradled it in her arms.

To her surprise, it made itself comfortable in her arms, making no move to jump or scratch at her, simply folding its ears onto its back. Eliza looked from the rabbit to the shed and back to the rabbit. Did it really want her to go in there? Or was it just a coincidence?

She shook her head before walking up to the old building. It looked as if it could collapse at any given time, leaning over to the right and with holes where there most likely were windows once. It looked haunted, but given the night she had just had, or dreamed at least, this did not frighten the girl. Walking into the shed took a bit more crouching and climbing than Eliza had expected. As she opened the shed's door, it fell apart in front of her, and she barely managed to jump out of the way, clutching the shaking rabbit close. Once inside, Eliza looked at what she had found. Some old working tools, most likely for the garden, all gathered in so much dust and cobwebs, that she feared it would coat her whole jumper and she would never get it off. She had to bend her head as she walked, for even for an 11-year-old, the ceiling was low and there were cobwebs hanging all around.

Turning around and taking in all the curiosities she found, Eliza started to look at one of the low shelves. There were old, cracked flowerpots, gardening tools and what seemed to be a small chest crammed in the back. With one hand, the other still holding on to the rabbit for fear it would run around and hurt itself on a piece of broken pottery or a nail from the fallen door, Eliza drew the chest out and placed it on the floor. It too, unsurprisingly, was covered in layers of dust. It looked to be about the size of a book, and not very thick either, with a small clasp in the front where one would put a small lock. Thankfully, it was lock free, so she opened it. There were a lot of papers, most so old they couldn't be read, written in beautiful cursive Eliza had never seen anyone write in, so it must be quite old. She tried to read some of them, but they were mostly gibberish or declarations of love or other types of nonsense that grownups wrote. She placed them on the floor beside her before looking back into the box. There, no, she must have seen wrong, for Eliza swore she saw- No it was, an old picture! Squinting, she could barely make out the people on it. There was a tall man in a top hat, and two women, one sitting and the other standing beside him. Eliza gasped before dropping the picture. It couldn't be, but it was. In that old photo, as real as she was, she recognised her ghosts, her friends, from her dream. It wasn't a dream, it was real, it had to be for next to the photo lay what looked like a chip, a chip from a teacup, with light blue embroidery. There were other photos lying underneath, but Eliza paid them no mind, her eyes fixed on the photo on the ground.

"Oh, silly rabbit." Eliza lowered the chip back into the chest before closing and placing it back where she had found it.

"What to do now?"

Chapter 7
A Rabbit's Journey

The trail back to her grandparents' house seemed longer to Eliza, since she didn't need to run and she hugged the seemingly sleeping rabbit close as she weaved her way out of the woods and into the open part of the garden. How long had she been away? The sun shone just as brightly and the air had lost its chill, so it had been a while, Eliza reckoned, and she hoped her grandparents hadn't noticed her absence because they liked to keep her within eyesight. They forgot often enough, and Eliza enjoyed the freedom it gave her, for she never liked to be watched, especially by her grandfather's stern gaze, as he liked to comment on her 'boyish' appearance and rowdiness. He wanted her to act more like the young lady he saw her as, and not the independent girl she was.

Eliza never cared about what she wore, be it a summer dress or torn jeans, if she could do what she wanted, like climb the highest trees and beat the other teams in football, she would be happy. Her mother had told her once, after a teary shouting match with her grandparents after she had muddied the new dress her grandmother had made her, that her grandfather just didn't know better since he was from a different time.

"Well, he's living in my time now, and shouldn't yell about stuff he's too old to understand!" Eliza had yelled before running to her room, stomping her feet every other step.

No, it had served her better to be left alone when she played outside.

She hurried to her room and changed her clothes before her grandfather saw the state of the old ones. Slowly walking into the foyer, pulling off her rainboots she made a beeline for the stairs, Eliza hoped she would go unnoticed. Luck seemed, however, not to be on her side that day. Just as she was about to start climbing the stairs, she heard her grandmother calling from the kitchen, Eliza wondered if she had been there since she left earlier, she probably had, too.

"Just where do you think you are going with that wild creature, Elizabeth Roberts?" Her grandmother's voice was cold and sharp like an ice shard.

Eliza squeezed her eyes shut, muttering a curse under her breath before turning towards the kitchen door where her grandmother now stood.

"I found it in the woods, it showed me an old shed a little while off the path! I think it wanted me to explore it, and I picked it up, and now it wants to stay! Can I keep it? Just while I'm here, and I'll feed it every day, oh please Grandmother, can I?" Eliza's plea seemed for a moment to fall on deaf ears, then the old woman smiled mischievously before lowering herself to the young girl's height. It's seemed as if the old woman hadn't heard Eliza mentioning the shed, for she continued to smile, gazing lovingly at the animal.

"You know, I had a small flock of rabbits when I was a young girl, and I kept them hidden away from my parents, and then later from my husband. Your grandfather is usually a nice man, but he sees these little creatures as pests, and would have shot them all if given the chance. So, you can keep it, but only for tonight, then it's up to your parents, and I doubt they will take as kindly to it as I have, dear!"

Eliza couldn't contain her smile. It shone as brightly as the sun outside as she leapt to her grandmother's side, hugging her as tightly as she could with the rabbit in her arms. It gave a squeak, as if surprised by the sudden movement, and seemed to glare up at the young girl holding it.

"Now, go change your clothes before your grandfather sees you, and wash your face while you're at it. You seem to have some dirt on your cheeks! Whatever were you doing in those woods?" Her grandmother's words barely reached Eliza who had already bolted up the stairs. She had nearly reached her bedroom before the old woman noticed her absence.

Slamming the door shut with her back before leaning on it, Eliza tried to calm her breath. Looking down at the rabbit still calm in her arms, she traced two fingers between its ears in a soothing rhythm, marvelling at its soft fur and long ears that laid down its brown and grey back, breathing out as her fingers trailed down again and again. Had she not known better, it would seem like their breath came at the same time as their eyes connected. Surely this was no ordinary wild rabbit, so tame and friendly. Otherwise, it would have tried to claw its way from her the moment she picked it up, yet it didn't. Eliza bent down and placed the rabbit on the floor a few steps in front of her before lying down, never losing eye contact as she crossed her arms before her and rested her head atop of them.

"What are you, really? You can't be a wild rabbit, but why would anyone release such a pretty thing out in the woods I don't know…" She paused, as if waiting for an answer from the creature staring back at her, so concentratedly. "Well, you're mine now anyway, so you don't have to worry about being alone ever again! — yet I can't keep calling you silly rabbit, now can I?"

Scrunching up her face, tilting her head to the right and swishing her legs behind her, Eliza thought hard. It couldn't be a normal bunny name, like Snowball, Fluffy or Thumper, for this was no ordinary bunny. Minutes ticked by in the same manner as it always did, Eliza thought, the rabbit twitching its nose and sometimes flicking one ear, the only sound being Eliza's legs as they crossed. Giving out a humph of annoyance and letting her legs fall to the floor with a thud, sending the rabbit running for cover under the bed in the corner at the opposite side of the room, Eliza turned so she was lying on her back, glaring up at the ceiling.

"I give up!" She announced to no one in particular. "Unless you have any ideas, rabbit, I'm afraid you won't have a new name yet, for it can't be just anything, you know, it needs to be special." The rabbit poked its head out from under the bed to look back at the girl.

Then Eliza's face lit up like someone had turned on a lightbulb in her head.

"I know, maybe my new friends will know what to call you! Oh, you'll love them, rabbit, they are the kindest ghosts I've ever met, well, the only ghosts I've met, but I'm sure they'll love you!" Eliza stood up and walked over to the shelf containing all the books she had brought with her over the years; books that she had gotten too old for or read years ago but cherished and would never grow tired of. Looking at the covers, trying to decide what to read, she read them out loud to herself.

"*Pippi Long stockings*, *Around the World in 80 Days*, *Winnie the Pooh*, *Harry Potter and the Philosopher's Stone*, *A Series of Unfortunate Events* and *The Hungry Caterpillar*." Eliza looked at the rabbit who had managed to drag the blanket on the bed down onto the floor, where he now lay, flop sided on top of it, looking rather pleased with itself.

"You look comfortable," Eliza giggled, one hand reaching for a book, the other on her hip, reminding herself of her grandmother when she scolded grandfather for snoring during their TV time.

Looking back at the books, she glided her hand across the backs of the hardcovers. Books had always been meaningful for Eliza. Growing up she had learnt to read as quickly as she could, and the nightly stories her parents had read to her became her time to read to them.

Then she wanted to read them to herself at night as it went faster if she didn't have to read them out loud. In the end, her parents had to set a timer, checking in on her an hour after bedtime to make sure she had stopped reading and gone to bed. Most nights she hadn't.

Smiling to herself, Eliza picked out, *Around the World in 80 Days*. The old hardcover gave an audible creak as she opened it before turning around and sitting on the blanket on the ground, next to the rabbit. Her hand went down in search of the creature, petting it slowly as her eyes wandered over the page. She wondered if it would like to hear the story, concluding that it most likely would, and so she started to read out loud.

"Mr Phileas Fogg lived, in 1872, at Nr. 7, Savile Row, Burlington Gardens, the house in which Sheridan died in 1814."

Several hours later, rising from her curled up position on the floor where she had fallen asleep, Eliza heard her grandma shouting from downstairs. It was time for dinner. She rubbed the sleep from her eyes before stretching, stifling a yawn, glancing briefly down towards the still sleeping rabbit as she stood up. The clock on her nightstand told her it was just past six in the evening, how the time had slipped by so quickly, she had no idea. Padding down the stairs she reminded herself to ask for some raw carrots and broccoli (her grandmother never made a meal without them) to give to the rabbit. Some old newspapers too, she didn't want droppings all over.

Dinner was something Eliza never looked forward to at her grandparents' house. It was usually unappetising, and this time was no different; something akin to meat that felt too gooey and too dry at the same time, boiled potatoes that fell apart if you looked at them wrong, and as Eliza had guessed, boiled carrots. She had pushed the food around her plate for an appropriate amount of time before excusing herself. Grabbing a few uncooked carrots she ran back upstairs, ranting about getting back to her book. Her grandparents looked at each other, neither really understanding what had just happened.

Eliza spent most of the evening reading, feeding the rabbit and petting it and looking hopefully at the clock, before starting all over again. She kept gnawing on her bottom lip until she felt a copper tang in her mouth and she realised she had pierced it. It was only nine o' clock, but Eliza had changed back into her nightgown and donned her only pair of woollen socks. They were a horrible mix of green, red, blue, yellow and purple, as if a knitting machine had exploded and they were made in the process. Yet it was not an accident that made those strange things, it was her grandmother, so Eliza wore them with a small sense of pride, for there was no one else who had such socks, ugly as they were. They were hers and hers alone.

As she stood by the wardrobe, admiring the socks, she tried to tame her curls with an ornate comb that belonged to her great grandmother. It was polished to look as if it were made of silver and had pearl inlaid across its back. She cradled it in her hands. Oh, how scared she was of breaking it. It had nearly snapped last night when she had used it, and now that her curls were in need of it, she wouldn't use it. Her grandmother would have a fit if she broke it, it being so old and all. No, her hair would go unkempt and wild another day. Instead, half of it got pulled up in a bun while the rest flowed free down her shoulders. She wasn't planning on sleeping tonight, and who knew, maybe they would dance again? So, best to keep the hair out of the way. Eliza looked herself over with stern eyes before nodding. She was ready.

Eliza hadn't meant to fall asleep, on the contrary, she had fully planned on staying awake until just before midnight, then she and her rabbit would sneak back up to the attic and meet her new friends again. However, fall asleep she did. Half lying, half sitting with her back towards the bedpost on the floor because the bed had been much too comfortable and Eliza feared she'd fall asleep. The rabbit lay asleep on her lap and her head lolled back on the bed. She awoke with a panicked grunt. Realisation hit her and she searched frantically for the clock. It was ten minutes to midnight. She stood up so abruptly that the rabbit, only half awake itself, tried to hold on to her thigh with a mad passion, and subsequently managed to rip a tear in Eliza's nightgown before she could grab a hold of it. She let out a yelp as claws connected with bare skin under the gown before she could stop herself. Pulling the rabbit up and pressing it to her chest, she mumbled sweet nothings to it, trying to calm it down as she fought the tears threatening to spill from her eyes. There was no time to lose, for who knew how long the ghosts would remain visible to her, if they were even there at all?

Padding as quietly across the floor, tripping along to the ballet playing in her head — for had her cry not awoken her grandparents, a creaky floorboard would; but the added weight of the rabbit, her tears blurring her eyes and the race against the clock made it more difficult to move. She was out of the door and started to move more quickly over the hardwood floor, hoping that she would make it, that she would see her friends once more. Then she was at the stairs; one, two, three at a time. She would make it! Her foot slipped and Eliza, whose weight was leaning forward, landed hard with her right foot on the second to last step. The sound of angry old wood being mistreated could be heard out in the streets, or so Eliza felt.

Her heart stopped as she listened, but knowing she didn't have the time to wait, she carried on up. Just as her fingers closed around the doorknob to the attic, there came a sound from below.

"Eliza, is that you dear?"

Her grandmother! It was her grandmother, she must have heard her sneaking out, or the door closing, or the step in the staircase. Eliza didn't dare breathe. Her fingers worked as silently as they could, turning the knob slowly, slowly, almost there. It opened. The door had opened a centimetre before she stopped it, knowing it's creak would give away her position immediately. No sound came from downstairs, had the old lady gone back to her bed? Would she check hers? Then a shuffling, a click and then silence.

Right, Eliza thought. *Time to move.* She opened the door as calmly yet as quickly as she could with one hand, one ear on the door and the other on the hallway below. Five centimetres, ten, *Almost there,* she thought, twenty centimetres, she could almost squeeze in, thirty-five — *Yes.* Eliza hugged the rabbit close before slipping inside and closing the door behind her.

"I thought I heard your rowdy steps coming up here." Eliza looked up as Victoria's shadow emerged from behind the wardrobe, first clouded then fuller, as though her body turned from a picture to a living -dead- being.

Eliza gave the older woman her biggest smile as she walked towards her then, letting the rabbit down beside her.

"Oh, Victoria, I was wondering if I would see you again, you see, I fell asleep and when I woke up, it had gotten so late and I'm not sure what time I can see you. Is it only at night that we- at least I- can see the ghosts?" Eliza was rambling, twisting her fingers together to calm herself down.

Victoria looked at the girl, her small, almost catlike eyes blinking rapidly as the girl talked. Gerald, accompanied by Anne, appeared beside her shortly after Eliza had started talking. They now looked towards the older woman quizzically, but she just gave them a raised eyebrow in reply before turning her attention back to the girl. Gerald tried to follow as the girl started to tell Victoria about her day and her discoveries, his eyes never leaving her; intrigued even though he had a hard time understanding some of it, he gave her his undivided attention. The same could not be said for Anne. The younger woman floated down into a chair, listening to Eliza with a playful smile tugging at her lips, her dark curls, so much like Eliza's own, falling way past her shoulders, almost into her lap. She sometimes longed to style it up like she had when she was alive, like Victoria's were, but it had been loose when she died and loose it would remain as long as she existed. Her mind had wandered to the old popular styles of her youth when her eyes caught a glimpse of something furry scuttling along the edge of a broken couch beside Eliza. It couldn't be, could it? It must be! Anne shot upwards with a squeal of delight, floating over to the couch, bending down to reach underneath, and pulled out a big, brown, fluffy rabbit.

"Ms Áine!" Anne exclaimed as she twirled herself and the rabbit around and around the attic.

Victoria looked at the her as if she'd gone mad. Gerald looked equally humoured and worried. Eliza however didn't know what was happening. Why was Anne twirling her wild rabbit around, calling it Áine? It was too much to think about, so she just stood there, mouth agape, staring, wondering what the older woman was doing. Anne didn't seem to mind. She was pressing the rabbit close, kissing it, twirling again, rubbing her nose to its nose.

"Anne, dear, care to tell us what exactly you are doing with that-that rodent?" Victoria scrunched-up her nose, looking as if she smelled something foul, and pointing a dainty finger towards the rabbit clenched tightly in Anne's arms.

"This is just like when we were alive and you made a pet out of one of cook's rabbits! Honestly Anne, you don't know where that thing has been." Victoria stopped, her glance shifting from the smiling Anne - who seemed oblivious to her tirade; and over to Eliza who had plumped down, crossed her legs, and started thinking. Seeing that the girl was lost in her mind, she continued. "Put it back where you found it. Hopefully, the girl's grandfather will find it and release it back outside, if not make dinner out of it!" She crossed her arms defiantly.

At this, Anne looked up, a horrified look on her face, mouth open in a silent refusal. Pulling the rabbit, Ms Áine, as she called it, defensively to her chest, as if she were afraid it would be taken from her. Gerald floated between the two women, shaking his head and waving his hands towards them in what he assumed was a gentle, calming manner.

"Ladies, ladies, let's not get our knickers in a twist!"

Wrong thing to say, for now both Anne and Victoria stared at him, anger seeping from their voices as they shouted at the man. Anne in indignation trying to get them to listen, while Victoria; angrier at being talked to in that way, seemingly having forgotten about the rabbit, started to lecture the poor man in decency, saying how rude it was to butt into other people's conversations, especially those he didn't have anything to do with. When he meekly answered that he was going to have to live with the two women quarrelling, so it was, in fact, his business as well, he almost lost his hat when Victoria's arms started to fly around as her temper rose.

Having been watching from the floor, slightly alarmed yet also fascinated with the arguments taking place in front of her, Eliza took matters into her own hands. She stood up, cleared her throat and lifted the rabbit out of Anne's arms before she let out a loud, high-pitched whistle. The ghosts made for the hills.

Having forgotten the girl altogether, the whistle came as a surprise, especially coming from a young lady, and they floated as quickly as they could. Gerald almost jumping over the broken couch, Victoria hid in the large wardrobe while Anne crouched behind the gramophone, still highly visible to Eliza, who fought a wild laugh tearing at her throat, begging to be let out. She stifled it but let out a harsh breath through her nose.

Slowly, the ghosts re-emerged, Gerald's head poked up from the couch, Victoria leaned out of the side of the wardrobe and Anne floated up from underneath the gramophone. However, she fitted underneath the small music player. Eliza probably didn't know much about ghosts' logic. — Then, they were all in front of her again, looking rather sheepish, as if they had been caught trying to steal sweets from the kitchen.

"Would someone care to tell me what's going on here?" Eliza asked. Exasperated as Eliza looked, her main feeling was curiosity. She hoped the ghosts would tell her the truth. They gathered in front of her, Anne closest, her eyes never leaving the rabbit, as she started talking.

"Many years ago, when I was alive, when I had just moved in with Victoria in this house after Gerald had passed, I saved a rabbit from our cook's garden, it was the last live rabbit, and I kept it as a pet. I gave it an Irish name. It means lucky one, for that's what she is, lucky.

I argued a lot with dearest Victoria over her, but in the end I got to keep her. I had the rabbit for a long time until one afternoon during summer, as we were relaxing out in the garden, a murder of crows shot out and scared the poor thing enough to make her bolt right into the woods! I looked for her for hours until Victoria all but dragged me back inside." Anne gave a haughty look at her older friend, who in turn just sniffed as she turned her nose upwards.

"You see, Eliza dear, your rabbit there looks just like my lost Áine. She even has the same clever expression in her eyes, as if she recognises me." Anne's voice turned shaky, as if she were holding back tears. "I-I know it can't be her, not really, but for one moment I had her back." The tears ran slowly down Anne's cheek.

Eliza got the feeling that it wasn't just about the rabbit, but she let it go, pleased with what she had heard. So, the night continued, tea and stories flowed and laughter rang clear up under the ceiling of the attic. Especially when Gerald told them about the time in his childhood, when he and a boy he knew would climb up on the roof of his parents' estate to see who could spit the longest, until one day he had managed to hit the town's vicar who had stopped by for tea. After that day, he was forbidden to climb the roof, and his bottom had stung for three days.

Eliza shared the story of last Christmas when she had woken up before anyone else and had gone down to look at the presents. She had also made a stop by the kitchen. There she found a bowl filled with heavenly chocolates, precious sweets and enticing caramels. She had been very clever when taking some, unwrapping each one and replacing them with grapes and raisins so her parents wouldn't see. They found out, of course, and she had suffered a tummy ache all day long and had not been allowed to have any pudding. The night went quickly and Eliza had hoped they would dance once more, seeing that she would be leaving the following day, but no such luck. She let out a yawn before leaning towards Anne.

"I'll tell you what, since it's my last night, I'll let Áine stay here with you tonight." Eliza hadn't finished talking before she found herself engulfed in a hug.

It was the strangest hug she had ever encountered for it felt as though her body was engulfed by the lightest blanket, yet she felt it squeeze her with a mighty force. Closing her eyes she could feel the woman's arms around her back, yet they were as soft as feathers. Then it was gone, and before Eliza opened her eyes she knew she would be alone.

And as the clock in the hall downstairs chimed midnight, the girl looked out into the empty attic and smiled, saying, "Good night, my friends."

Chapter 8
The Portal

It was raining. That much was clear. The rhythmical tap, tap, tap-ing on the window sounded muted, although audible, behind a thick curtain. Had Eliza not been asleep already, the sound would have helped her drift off, but now it woke her up. The first thing she noticed, besides the fact that it was raining, was that lying beside her, partially under the covers, was the rabbit. How had it ended up back here? It couldn't have jumped down all those stairs and opened her bedroom door all by itself now could it? It didn't make sense, yet if she was being honest with herself, noting that had happened this weekend did. She had met ghosts, talked to them and even danced! It must all be real. Then a thought struck her.

"I can't tell anyone about this weekend, can I, silly rabbit?" Eliza wondered, stroking its soft fur.

Who would believe her, even if she found someone to tell about her discoveries? She couldn't tell her parents; they wouldn't believe it, and it was not as if they listened to her stories nowadays anyway. Her few friends in school would think she was weird, seeing stuff that wasn't there. They might even chase her away; not wanting to be friends with someone who talked to ghosts. Then a frightening thought struck her; what if some adults found out, and they would demand to see them, talk to them or worse, take them away? No it was quite clear, this would forever be her secret, and she would keep it with honour. A shout came from downstairs, her grandmother calling to inform her about breakfast, it was time to get dressed. Eliza wanted nothing more than to get the goodbyes over with. She hated goodbyes.

Blue and white cat sweater on, jeans and wool socks wrestled with and hair placed securely in a ponytail, Eliza was ready, physically at least. Her gaze drifted towards the attic; up the stairs, to the door, over and under furniture, towards the little group sitting there on the old picnic table drinking tea. Eliza wondered if they would miss her, but she was just being foolish. She would come back soon and see them again, then she would tell them about her adventures!

Gerald's eyes would gleam with mischief when she regaled him about her fights with the boys, Victoria would heave a sigh of discontent or harumph as she wrinkled her nose when Eliza would tell of matches won on the football field. Anne would probably want to hear about Áine and how spoiled the poor thing would be. So, she kept her head held high, for although this weekend had come to an end, there would be more. She would visit every other weekend if her grandparents allowed it. With her mind set, and hopes high, the young girl picked up her rabbit, giving it a light kiss before returning it to the blanket on the floor. It was time for breakfast, and she mustn't be late.

Breakfast went by in a daze. Eliza half listened to her grandmother argue about whether one could have too much tea in the morning, while her grandfather shook his head.

"Of course not, plumpy," his pet name for his wife. "Tea is healthy, and a growing child can never have enough!" His booming voice sounded sure as he gave a curt nod.

Eliza snickered as she overheard her grandmother mumble. *It was you I was worried about, not the child*, as Eliza rarely had more than a cup in the morning while her grandfather had at least three. She moved the scrambled eggs around her plate, making them more of a mush then scrambled. Eliza never really liked her eggs scrambled, they tasted like raw bread dough with too much salt. Looking between her grandparents, one leg bouncing rhythmically under the table, she hoped to be excused. Áine needed to be let outside for a little while before her father came to pick her up. She was already nervous about what he would say about the rabbit, so the thought of it leaving gifts in the back of his new car was out of the question. Her grandmother had noticed the girl's wandering mind and restless leg, and with a scrunch of her nose she excused Eliza from the table.

The rain had stopped, probably during breakfast, but the humidity hung in the air like a heavy blanket, frizzing the curls in Eliza's hair as soon as she stepped outside. The ground was muddy and slippery beneath her feet as she trudged slowly through the garden and towards the woods. The rabbit, usually calm in her arms, started to twist around, claws digging into the sleeve of her sweater in a frantic need to escape. Eliza yelped as one of the creature's claws dug painfully through the fabric and into her arm, sending the animal to the ground. She hurried to pick it up, wanting to be sure it hadn't been hurt by the fall, however it seemed that the rabbit had other plans. As soon as it landed, it darted away from her, under a bush, over a tree root and across the path. Eliza sprinted after it, calling out for it to stop, wait, or just to look back at her. She was terrified of losing it.

What would Anne say? She ran after it as best she could, jumping, ducking and clawing her way through the trees, always keeping Áine within eyesight.

She could feel her sweater ripping in a place near her shoulder as she barrelled through a heavy thorn bush and her eyes stung with unshed tears. Then, in the same manner as it had done the first time they met, the rabbit stopped. This time, instead of stopping in front of a shed, the animal stood still in front of what looked to be an opening. Around them, most of the threes had thinned out, leaving a small clearing. Eliza didn't believe her eyes. She blinked, once, twice, rubbed them for good measure, but it didn't go away. Right in front of the rabbit, nestled between a grand pine tree and some moss covered rocks, hanging in the middle of the air, was an opening. Eliza didn't know what else to call it, for it was just that, an opening into another forest.

She knew it was a different place, for trickling through the hole in the air, came rain slowly drizzling. A sense of dread filled the child as she stood in front of it.

We should run away! Came a voice from the back of her mind, but before she could think to answer another shouted, *No, we must see where it leads!* Eliza felt as if she was pulled in two directions by invisible threads, both strong enough to tear her apart, it seemed.

She was about to act when suddenly the rabbit squeaked, as if to get her attention, then started to move closer to the opening. She didn't think, instead Eliza moved after it, wanting to grab it before it could jump through, but she was too late. For as her fingers closed around the warm body of the rabbit, she had the unmistakable feeling of rain falling on her head.

It was a mistake. As soon as she felt the rain on her face, she knew she shouldn't be there. Yet as her head swam, her eyes took in the fog surrounding the small patch of woods before her, and she moved forward; each step carefully placed in front of the other as the surrealism of it all hit her. Casting a glance behind her to the opening they had just entered, she could still see the moss covered ground and the sun starting to light it up. Eliza pulled the rabbit; now calm once again close to her chest before looking straight ahead again. Curiosity grew in her stomach, outshining the terrified butterflies that lingered until it became all she felt.

"We should go back." It came as more of an answer than a statement as she took in the calm morning so different from the one she had left. Yet when she started to move, it was towards the trees and not back through the opening.

"I wonder, silly rabbit, where we would end up if we kept on walking?" Áine gave no reply, instead he burrowed his face into the girls arms, content and calm.

The forest path on this side of the opening was less overgrown, though trees, bushes and rocks stood unwavering around them, they seemed younger in a way; less bushy and crowded. Eliza stepped carefully ahead, eyes scanning around, trying to take in all that she saw in case she needed to find her way back in a hurry. Something felt off to her. Everything seemed so familiar. Then she saw it; there, was that, was that a house glinting between the trees? Yes, it was! It was her grandparents' house! Eliza sprinted closer, not letting the house out of her sight, and subsequently, she didn't notice how much more well-kept the garden seemed, with strange flowers starting to wilt in the cold. Her father would soon be here to pick her up, and she had no idea how long she had been away, and fearing his anger at being kept waiting, she kept running towards the back door. As she reached it, she meant to fling it open and yell out *I'm here!* And *No need to worry!* Yet, as her hand closed around the doorknob, yanking on it to open, she found the door locked, unwilling to budge.

Stunned, Eliza looked at it, the back door was never locked during the day when she was visiting. It must be her grandmother's old mind that had forgotten that she was outside and had locked it out of habit. Using her one free hand, Eliza started to bang on the door, calling out for her grandparents to open it, yet no reply came. The sound of heavy breathing was the only sound to be heard in the garden. Then footsteps could be heard from the other side of the door. Eliza's face lit up as she heard the door unlock, yet her face fell when she saw who opened the door. There, standing in front of her, in what looked to be a well-tailored suit that people wore on the TV, stood a man. Not her grandfather, not her father, but an older man she had never seen before.

"What is the meaning of such a ruckus, child?" The man's voice was cold and unfriendly, as if he were talking to a door-to-door salesman or a rat. His nose turned up haughtily as he looked down at the girl and took in the torn trousers, the scratches on her face and the twig that had got stuck in her hair.

Eliza couldn't do much else than stare up at the man. The look he gave her made her feel as unwelcome as if he had slammed the door in her face. She tried to answer him, yet found no words, although her mouth hung open.

"Well? Tell me your business this instant or I shall have to inform the police!" His tone felt like ice, and the words made Eliza want to run as far away as she could.

"I-I'm looking for my grandparents, they live here…" Eliza trailed off, for as she said it, she knew in her heart that her grandparents did not live here, not yet at least.

The look on the old man's face told her as much, but before he could answer her, a woman's voice sounded from behind him, and Eliza's heart filled with longing. She knew that voice.

"Mr Holden, what is the meaning of this? You are letting all the warmth out. Either invite the person in or send them on their merry way!" The voice could belong to no one else, and as Eliza tried to see behind the old man, the owner of the voice appeared.

"Victoria! Oh, Victoria, it's you! Please let me in, I have no idea how I ended up here, and I need your help." The calm that had taken place in Eliza vanished as soon as she saw the woman fully.

This was not the ghost woman she knew. This Victoria was alive, clad in a black gown with laces and ruffles, and looked so much like the one she had been wearing when they had danced that Eliza first thought she was dreaming. Her blonde hair was pinned tightly in an updo, not a strand out of place, her face pale yet pink hues filled her cheeks. Her eyes, a clear blue. Eliza looked at her with confusion and uncertainty. She had no idea who the girl was.

"That's Mrs Hardbrook to you, girl!" The man's voice cut through Eliza and Victoria's staring, making the young girl jump and the older woman scowl.

"No need Mr Holden, the child must be delusional, send her away and close the door, I have other matters to attend to, as do you." With a final glance at her, eyes piercing into the girl, Victoria turned around and walked back into the house. Eliza's pleas falling on seemingly deaf ears.

"You heard the missus, on your way then!" Mr Holden shooed with violent hands, as if afraid to touch the girl and slammed the door as quickly as he could.

Eliza stood frozen to the staircase, slightly trembling, and her arm holding the rabbit, who had remained calm during the ordeal. Her arm felt numb from the weight.

What on earth had just happened? Slowly walking away from the doorstep, Eliza started to think, failing to notice the way her feet carried her. *Why was Victoria here? How was she alive? Where are my grandparents?* Fear started to creep into the girl's bones, coming to the conclusion that she must no longer be in her own time any more. Why else would Victoria be here? Unless she was still dreaming.

As thoughts ran around, some more peculiar than others, the street beneath Eliza's feet turned from grass and gravel to cobblestones. The open countryside with it's big trees and rolling hills gave way to more and more houses. The sound of footsteps, wheels and people talking could be heard all around, yet they went unnoticed by the child; so lost was she in her mind. Then, as quickly as she had been walking, she stopped.

"This can't be real, Áine, I must still be in my bed, and any minute now, Grandma will be calling us down for breakfast!" Eliza said with a confidence she dared not feel, eyes never leaving the rabbit in her arms.

Just as she was about to continue walking, something collided with her, subsequently falling to the ground with a thud and a loud yelp.

"Hey, look where you're going!" Eliza shouted just as she saw who she had run into.

There, on the ground that was no longer a forest floor, her grandparents yard or driveway — but rather a cobblestoned sidewalk — lay a boy, a few years older than Eliza. His clothes, torn and dishevelled, looked to be about twice his size. They also looked like nothing Eliza had ever seen anyone wear. Trousers made from what looked to once have been a flour sack, with a hole at the right knee and tied together with a string around his ankles. His shirt -which Eliza thought looked more like an old curtain than a shirt, was half tucked in, half hanging out of his trousers with what seemed to be a wool vest keeping it from hanging open, was a lovely shade of dirt brown. He had fallen back yet had managed to turn, landing face down. He turned towards Eliza, eyes screwed shut in pain, as his right hand went towards his head, holding tight to his right side. On his hands he wore fingerless old gloves and his shoes seemed to be the only items that were not too big, but rather slightly too small. His hair was jet black and thick as fur with white stripes just above his left eyebrow. As he removed his hand, Eliza saw what he had been pressing on.

"Oh my, you seem to have gotten a cut!" Without thinking, Eliza leaned down in front of the boy, one hand holding the rabbit while the other reached out for the injury.

"Get your hand off me! I don't need no dumb girl messing with my face!" His voice was angry, although Eliza could hear the strain in it, so, seeing the tears threatening to fall from his eyes, she said nothing.

His eyes, oh she had never seen such blue eyes. The irises were clearer than the lightest summer sky, almost white, with a darker ring containing them from spilling out and joining the milky white of his eye. His lip trembled as he looked down at his hand now covered in blood and his face paled. Eliza knew she should get an adult and looked up to see if she could find one, but what she saw had her frozen to the ground.

All around them people were walking, talking, shopping, stressing, shouting and living. Yet Eliza had never felt so much in a dream as she did then. Nothing was familiar. The few houses that had surrounded her grandparent's house — the old suburban family houses and apartments were nowhere to be seen. Instead rickety buildings built almost on top of each other stood leaning against one another, all in murky brown, grey and black stone. The people walking around them, taking no notice of the confused children were dressed in big gowns; some nice, some tattered and some in nothing but rags. Men in suits walked about as if they were all heading to weddings or funerals, looking sombre and mean. Then, at the corner of the street stood a horse and carriage, as if their rightful place was in the middle of the street and they had been parked there for a reason.

A whimper drew Eliza out of her confusion. The boy on the ground looked up at her, fear clear in his heavenly eyes, and a wave of protectiveness rushed over the girl. She would take care of him. Yet, she needed answers, so before she could care for him, she needed to know what she already feared herself.

"Tell me, what year is it?" Eliza asked her voice trembling.

"Why, it's 1889 of course!"

Chapter 9
1889

Ice ran through her veins instead of blood. Her stomach dropped as she swallowed and her breath came out as fog as his words settled. It wasn't real, how could it be? Eliza's eyes flew about trying to find something to prove him wrong; a car, a person with a phone, someone dressed normally, anything. The more her eyes took in, the more terror filled her body and she couldn't stop the small cry that fell from her lips. Time stopped, the air stood still and the ground moved about her at a dizzying pace. The slap came out of nowhere and landed right on her cheek. It stung.

"Sorry about that, but you seemed ready to drop…" An uncertain voice said. It had come from the young boy who now stood close to Eliza.

Her eyes fixated on him, and in doing so, she found her balance and the world stopped spinning. Then she noticed her breathing slowing down. When had it picked up? There was a scratching noise, and Eliza looked down at the rabbit in her arms, now struggling to get away from her too tight grip. She loosened her hold and it calmed down.

"Why are you walking around with that thing?" The boy pointed a gloveless finger at the animal.

"I'm keeping it safe for a friend, but that's none of your business!" Eliza straightened herself up and met the boy's curious eyes with a fierce glare. "Now, I have no idea how I got here, and I have no idea how to get back. I don't belong here, you see-" Before she could finish, the boy interrupted her with a high voice.

"You don't belong here, all right! Never seen anyone looking like you do, in those clothes you could've been from the moon and I wouldn't have believed ya!" As he said it, his eyes roamed over Eliza with a mix of suspicion and curiosity.

"Never mind how I look. I need help getting back, and the only people I know here don't remember me! Or, they haven't met me yet…" The boy looked ready to say something but Eliza just held up a finger to silence him. "And without their help, I don't know if I'll ever get back, and I have people waiting for me!" Eliza had to fight the tears from spilling from her eyes. It was no use crying in front of the boy. He would probably just laugh at her or call her a sissy. Then she remembered his injury. "But first, let me help you with that wound on your face, before you say anything." She put her free hand up in the air to seem as non-threatening as possible. "You won't get cooties or anything from me, but you might get an infection if you let that go unchecked!"

He seemed ready to argue with her, before slowly shaking his head as he stepped closer. Eliza took a closer look at the cut. It wasn't as deep as she had first thought, and didn't seem to need stitching, but did, however, need to be cleaned and dressed. She was almost sure the boy would know of a place with clean water and maybe a towel to dress it with.

"Is there a place we could go that has clean water and maybe some clean rags?" The boy scoffed at her and gave her a look that clearly stated how dumb a question that was.

"Yeah, let's just run up to the nearest house and ask them for some water and rags to lend out to two street urchins they hardly know. Next thing you know, the coppers are after us!"

Although his tone was light, albeit haughtily, Eliza was taken aback by his words. She thought about her next words carefully, not wanting to say the wrong thing and possibly alienate him.

"So, we won't do that, we'll just have to find at least some water and a rag of sorts somewhere." Eliza looked around them to the houses and shops lining the streets. Then she saw it; in between two houses, hanging high up, but not so high that they couldn't reach it, a string with a few shirts, cloths and what looked to be nightgowns hanging from two windows.

"There! We can grab one of those rags and use that, then all we need is some water." Pointing towards the string to show the boy, Eliza started to move. Then an arm grabbed hers.

"As good as an idea that is, we'll be spotted! There are people everywhere and I ain't about to get locked up over a stupid girl." Eliza let out a huff of indignation. He was right though. Then a new idea struck.

"We need a distraction! I'll go up to one of the houses and knock, asking for some water while you sneak up and grab it, then you hide behind the house and I'll meet you there, hopefully with the water!" The boy seemed to agree with her idea.

"Ok, but I'll go knock, you look so weird that they won't trust ya and then we're in trouble…" They locked eyes, clear blue meeting hazel before Eliza thrust out her hand towards him.

"Deal, and my name is Eliza Roberts. Thought you should know the name of the girl who gave you that cut." A corner of the boy's lips turned upwards as he gave her another once-over before taking her small hand in his cold one.

"All right then, and you should know the name of the boy who's gonna help ya out. I'm Lucas, Lucas Whitlock!" His voice sounded proud, and his handshake was firm. Eliza liked the boy already.

The crooked house of brick and wood leaned slightly to the right. If it was because of how it was built or by time, Eliza didn't know. The other house, the one the end of the string was attached to, leaned slightly to the left. Looking up towards the roofs there was little space between them, as if the houses leaned towards each other, looking for support, and at one point, they would meet and keep each other grounded. Or crash together, splintering down, ruining both houses. Had they been painted in bright colours they could have been taken straight out of an amusement park.

Eliza followed Lucas with her eyes as he walked confidently up to the door of one of the houses. Now, they had to move at the right time. Trying not to look too conspicuous as she closed in on the clothing line, Eliza had to keep herself from crouching down from eyesight. For although those in the house might not see her, the people on the street might have found it odd to see a child crawling on the cold ground between two houses.

The knock sounded, and Eliza had to dart the few last steps. Lucas' voice came from the door, muffled slightly by the beating of Eliza's heart pounding in her ear. She looked closely at the clothes before she found it. She snagged the rag off the line and scratched her nose as she inspected it. Although it looked to have been washed, it was far from new. Once white, it now looked nearing yellow, with a tear in the left corner and what seemed to be a slightly brown stain on the bottom end. Eliza let out a huff as she rolled her eyes. It would have to do. The slamming of a door told her time was up, and as she stuffed the rag under her sweater before darting close to the house wall, listening for the boy. Lucas ran across the opening between the two houses, not stopping to wait for her or tell her what had happened. Eliza picked up her feet and ran after him, not stopping when she heard a loud voice call out.

"Thieves! Stop them! Somebody!"

Lucas sped up and she had to give it her all to keep up with him. They ran farther into the city, crossing streets, shops and people. Never looking back and keeping a steady pace, the children went further and further away from the place they had first met. The sounds of the city were loud; the chattering folk, the *Clip Clop* of hooves on cobblestones and shouts from store owners filled their ears. Eliza barely had time to notice how far they had run before Lucas took a sharp right into an ally, coming to a stop and leaning on the brick wall. Eliza mirrored his action opposite him, breath heaving and feet aching.

Then, out of nowhere, she started laughing. Not a soft chuckle, nor a breathy giggle, but a full blown, hearty and heavy laugh. Lucas looked at her as if she had gone crazy before the laugh infected him too. They had to fight to stay upright as the laugh dragged on, fatigue starting to eat away at them and adrenaline seeping out with every breath they took.

"Why…" Eliza tried to ask in between laughter and breaths. "…Why did you run?" They had stopped laughing now. Eliza's feet gave out and she sagged to the ground.

"Well…" Lucas seemed just as out of breath as she was. "You run when you take something, or else you get caught!" He answered, giving her a look as if to say it was self-explanatory.

Eliza's eyes scanned the boy but saw nothing that hadn't been with him before. Áine gave a squeak, letting the children know she was still there, and not pleased with having been hauled around at such a pace. Eliza apologised to the rabbit before setting it down next to her, giving it an affectionate pat before returning Lucas's gaze.

"What did you steal this time, then?" She tried to make her voice sound stern, cold like her father's would have been, but curiosity thawed it.

Lucas slipped his hand inside his vest, and seemingly out of nowhere pulled out what looked like a small, flat, brown flask and shook it from side to side, a lopsided grin growing on his face. Pride and smugness evident in his eyes as he looked at her.

"You said we needed water, as well as a rag, so I got us some. Impressed?" Lucas asked.

The girl's eyes lit up before she could compose herself, excited that he had remembered what she had told him. Then she gave a hard glare.

"It's not nice to steal. I said we should ask for water, not take a whole flask!" Eliza crossed her arms as she continued to glare at the boy.

The look on Lucas' face in any other circumstance would have made her laugh. His cocky grin falling away, eyebrows knitting and arms falling limp to his side as his head tipped to the right, a look of complete bafflement etched across his face.

"You just. Helped me. Steal something!" He punctuated every two words while pointing a finger from the hand not holding the flask at her.

Eliza just huffed. A dirty old rag was NOT the same as someone's water flask, and she explained that, besides, the rag was for his wound, not hers. She would have to find someone and get help. It then dawned on her again. There was no one to ask for help. She was alone in a city, in a time unknown to her, and she had no idea how to get back. Eliza shut her mouth with an audible snap.

"Hey, are you all right?" Lucas' voice was low, yet Eliza jumped where she sat.

Nodding her head, Eliza cleared her throat before looking back at him. She gave the wound another glance. The bleeding seemed to have stopped, which was a good sign, and it didn't look like it had any dirt or gravel in it. She took the flask from the boy's hand, untwisting the top and dabbing some water on the rag, making sure it was damp before reaching up towards his forehead. He flinched once and instinctively Eliza lowered her hand a little as she sought out his clear blue eyes.

"It might sting a little, but I won't hurt you." Lucas shifted his gaze fast between her eyes, looking to see if she was telling the truth. He must have believed her, for he gave a short nod, giving her permission to continue.

As gently as she could, Eliza drew the rag across the wound, cleaning out the old blood as well as the new that flowed. For a second, she was afraid it had been deeper than she thought, for the new blood flowed rapidly. Uncertain of what to do, she pressed the now soaked rag into the wound hard. Lucas let out a hiss at the contact. Eliza winced and apologised. The silence drew out between them, neither knowing what to do, what to say to the other, but both had so many questions that burned inside of them. It was Lucas who dared to ask first.

"So, who are you, really? And why are you here?" Their eyes met as he asked and Eliza switched the hand holding the rag as she scooted closer to him.

A part of her wanted to tell him everything. About her grandparents' house, her friends that lived there, about the rabbit, the portal, and her world. Yet she feared that he would laugh, run away and leave her there, completely and utterly alone. It was too much. She looked into his crystal clear eyes and was surprised by the warmth she saw there, for although they looked to be cut from ice, they were warm, as if a fire burned inside them. With a shuddering breath, Eliza started to tell her story. She looked into his eyes for the entirety of the story, not wanting to let go of them, afraid she would stop speaking if they broke contact. At that moment, they were her lifeline.

As her words came to an end, to the point where they had met and she had understood she was no longer in her own time, Eliza felt the final remnants of a tear dropping from her chin. Her breathing came in shallow drags and she was shaking. Why was she shaking? Then, the most remarkable thing happened. Lucas took the hand not pressed to his forehead and clamped it in his own, stopping it from shaking. She took the rag away from the wound. It had stopped bleeding and looked better already.

"I believe you, I won't say you don't sound ridiculous, because you do, but I believe you; and I swear on my life that one way or another, I will get you back home." His voice was calm, but it held a certainty that Eliza wouldn't dream of questioning.

"You will?" Eliza asked.

"Hey, you helped me out, and us street rats gotta stick with those who help us!" Eliza gave a chuckle at his words. "You won't have to do this alone."

Chapter 10
Anne?

Anne Richards sat patiently in her garden, studying the flowers gently placed around her. She had a plan to paint them, and had started, yet the beauty surrounding her had ceased her movements. Her paint brushes rested now in different angles in her untidy updo, hair and brushes dangling all around her head. Anne liked to keep them in a place she knew wouldn't soil her clothes or the flowers, and her unmanageable mop of curls was just as good of a place as any, and that way she always knew where to find them. Most of the flowers had died of the cold winter air, yet some resilient primroses and pansies had taken up the fight and still looked beautiful in the grey light of day. She knew that the window for natural light was short, so she had been seated outside for an hour already, trying to get as much painting done as the ever darkening day would allow. Taking a deep breath and trying to move her already sleeping legs, Anne got up from her spot on the blanket she had placed down as she had started her painting. She had a habit of getting lost in nature, and often, Victoria -or Gerald- had had to drag her back inside so as not to catch her death of cold. There was something about the rawness of nature that left her breathless, and its unwillingness to be swayed by neither riches nor stature demanded her respect, and she gave it willingly. A breeze billowed her skirt about her as she stood, eyes closed and hands outstretched before her, breathing in the clear air. The door behind her opened and a voice called out.

"Anne, dear, will you come inside for tea? You have been out there painting forever!" It was Victoria calling her.

Anne couldn't help but smile at her dearest friend's plea, although she remained standing with her back to the door, eyes still closed.

"Tori, you know I can't resist the natural light for my paintings, and I *so* enjoy my alone time in the garden." This was met with a scoff and a short laugh.

"Whosoever is delighted by solitude is either a wild beast or a God, they say."

At this, she turned around, eyebrow raised and lips pursed.

"And who, may I ask, says that? Was it you?" She asked.

Victoria took a step forward out from the doorway and wrapped the shawl hanging on her shoulders tighter around her.

"No, I believe it was Aristotle actually… Never mind who said it, will you come back inside?"

The other woman sniffed. "Yes, all right, just give me a moment and I'll be right there Tori." Victoria gave a curt nod before walking back inside the house.

Anne sighed, shook her head and bent down to pick up her canvas when she heard steps coming from around the house. Without taking her eyes from where the sound had come, she straightened, letting the painting drop back down. The sound became louder, and then two children appeared. They didn't seem to notice her, as they crouched along the flower beds surrounding the house itself. They wore the oddest clothes; the boy, in what could only be described as old rags and too big pants. The girl, however strange, seemed to be the complete opposite -although boy-ish in her appearance, clean, hole-free and brightly coloured. Anne had never seen clothing in such fabric, and never on a girl. The sweater even had a cat sewn on it. *How odd* she thought to herself. She waited to see if the children noticed her. They seemed to be speaking in hushed voices, then the boy turned towards the girl and pointed a finger at her, saying loudly enough to be heard.

"This was YOUR plan!" The girl slapped his shoulder and shushed him, then, as if finally feeling the woman's eyes upon her, the girl turned her head quickly towards Anne, stopping dead in her tracks.

Anne and the children looked at each other, neither knowing exactly what to do, nor why the other was there at that moment. The girl looked as if she had seen a ghost. Colour drained from her face, with eyes growing wide. The boy looked like he expected a good lashing if he didn't turn and run for the hill. Then the girl stepped forward.

"…Anne?" Her voice sounded weak, and the question barely rose above a whisper, yet Anne heard it as if she had been shouting. Why did this little girl know her name?

"Anne, is that really you?" Again the girl asked, this time with more conviction and taking a step forward. It was then Anne noticed the animal in the strange girls arms.

All doubt fell away from the girl as she saw the joy and love etched on Anne's face when she saw the rabbit. The girl took a step, then another, before lifting the rabbit and holding it up as if showing it to Anne.

"I brought her here with me, or technically, she brought *me* along. I think she wanted to go home. Do you remember her?" The girl sounded unsure, but her face looked hopeful.

Of course Anne remembered her, the fuzzy animal she had helped escape the cook right after moving in with Victoria. The rabbit that had disappeared shortly after. She had been afraid the cook had found the rabbit and made away with it, but here it was, as alive as she was. Her Áine, her lucky rabbit.

"Oh my, it can't be, can it? Is that my little Ms Áine you're holding? Wherever did you find her?" Anne drew closer to the outstretched rabbit before taking it in her arms and pressing it close. Her heart filled with joy, knowing that it was safe and back home with her. Then she looked closer at the children. Her eyebrows furrowing as she inspected them.

"Now, I think you two have a story to tell. Why don't you come inside with me, and you can tell me all about it." Anne tried to keep her voice stern, but she never enjoyed being the tough one. That was usually Victoria's job.

"I hope you don't have any plans..." Eliza couldn't help uttering under her breath.

***

To Eliza, the house looked the same on the outside as she knew it would, possibly a little cleaner. Yet it was the same colour, light blue, it had the same amount of windows, 18, and it was surrounded by (albeit different) flowers all around the front. Vines grew up the side of the house, green and thick, and Eliza immediately wanted to test to see if she could climb them. Cobblestones led all the way from the streets up to the front door, and the beginning of the garden gate could be seen jutting out from the opposite side of where they were standing. They had stopped by the woods on the other side of the street, looking to see if the coast was clear. As she stood next to Lucas, she could feel her nervousness growing. If they were spotted, would they be chased away? *Most likely,* she thought. She gave the boy to her left a look, and then they started edging closer.

Eliza had not expected to see anyone in the garden. She had hoped they would be able to sneak around the house, unspotted, and make a dash for the woods on the other side. Had it not been for the fence surrounding the garden all around, they would have found a safer way through, but climbing it would be near impossible. They had to go in the same way she came out. So, when she saw Anne standing in the garden, right in front of the path she would have chosen, she froze. For a second, Eliza wanted to run up to the woman and throw her now shaking arms around her, using what most likely would be her only chance to feel her before going home. But this was not the same Anne who had smiled so sweetly at her in the attic or given her the dear rabbit. No, this Anne did not know her. This Anne was the same as Victoria. The woman looked at them with a curious expression, as if she had been looking for a while, trying to figure out what they were doing. Eliza felt the blood rush from her face as the woman's name slipped out in a question. Then, as she took a step forward, she asked again. After she spoke, she saw that Anne's eyes had fallen to the rabbit still clutched in her arms and the doubt she had felt flowed away as she continued speaking. To her surprise, a flicker of recognition showed in Anne's face and then the woman spoke to them.

"Now, I think you two have a story to tell, why don't you come with me inside, and you can tell me all about it." Anne's voice was just as Eliza remembered, and it warmed her whole body hearing it. But the words made her think

"Hope you don't have any plans." She muttered.

The boy looked from the woman, to Eliza, then back at the woman again, contemplating if it would be a wise choice to follow them inside. He had only met the girl today and from years of experience, didn't trust strangers. But Eliza wasn't a stranger any more. She had helped him, cleaned his wound and that wasn't something anybody had done for him before. No, he trusted Eliza, but the woman, Anne he remembered, he wasn't so sure about. So, when she suggested they go inside, he froze.

Eliza looked at Lucas, beckoning him forward with her free hand. When he made no move to follow, she sighed before taking his hand in hers and dragging him with her. Anne had started to walk, so the children had to run to catch up with her. As they stood before the door, Anne turned to the children and spoke.

"Now, I am quite curious about all of this, but I do believe it might be a little bit too much for my friend to understand. She is very nice, and I'm sure she won't mind me asking you in, but leave the talking to me, all right?" Her voice was light, just like it always was around Eliza, but it had an edge to it, making the children nod in understanding.

Eliza knew what she meant, having met Victoria already, and remembered how she had acted. She felt Lucas' hand in hers and she gave him a smile, hoping it would reassure him.

The inside of the house contrasted with the outside. Where the house had looked almost the same from the outside, Eliza couldn't believe it was her grandparent's' old, rundown hallway she was standing in. The dark heavyset door had not a scratch nor a line through its paint. There were massive columns reaching from the beginning of the stairs all the way up to the second floor. The walls were covered with oil paintings of seaside's, towns and fields in all shapes and sizes. Even the wall itself was different. Whereas in her grandparents' time, the natural wood stood clear and naked all through the hallway, here it was coated in a deep burgundy wallpaper, Eliza thought. A beautiful carpet covered the hardwood floors beneath the children's feet as they stood huddled just behind Anne.

Eliza saw Lucas eyeing the decorations with just as much nervous excitement as she had. Then a thought struck her. She should have known, it must be his first time seeing such a house from the inside, for he had no place to live, and certainly no TV to see old period movies on. She looked down at their hands still entwined and made a promise to herself in that moment, that whatever happened, she would make sure that when she left, Lucas would have someone to take care of him.

She was brought out of her thoughts by Anne's hushed voice telling them to move quietly into the living room on the other side of the stairwell, as she would go into the kitchen to talk to Victoria. The children walked as lightly and as quickly as they could, Eliza taking the lead. As soon as they had entered the living room, Anne's voice could be heard talking animatedly to someone. The room they were now in had been decorated in much the same fashion as the hallway, although the opulence was more stated. The furniture Eliza recognised, it looked like the old couch up in the attic back in her grandparents' time. It had, for a while, been in the parlour, but you weren't allowed to sit on it. Here, large chairs and couches draped in old floral patterns made of soft fabric and hard wooden backs arching in loops, turns and curves stood out for anyone to use. Even the tables were decorated with ornaments in white, gold and silver, with what looked to be golden leaves and vines draped around the legs. Rococo, she remembered her grandma had called it. The walls were decorated with paintings, portraits and tapestries. Above the fireplace in the corner there even hung two swords mounted across an open book made of stone. The entire room felt like a museum and it was unbelievably beautiful. Eliza wanted nothing more than to run up to the nearest couch and jump on it, running her hands all over the hardwood armrests and wood carvings, feeling the patterns in the fabric, maybe even jumping on it to test the bounce, but the now loud voices from next door told her they might already be in trouble, so, no need to push their luck. A glance at Lucas told her he was as puzzled about what to do as she was, so Eliza pulled him along towards the middle of the room, hoping to put some distance from the shouting adults.

"Eliza, what are we doing here? We should run out now that we have the chance! I ain't going to the Lock Up over this!" His voice was almost frantic as his eyes darted from Eliza to the hall they had come from.

"Now that we've gotten this far, we're not backing out of it. They won't call the police on us; they might even help us!" Although Eliza felt certain about her words, the worry Lucas felt transferred itself over to her.

She didn't know these people, not really, and even though Anne and Victoria had been friendly and kind to her, that was not them standing in the kitchen now, and those women Eliza didn't know at all. She was staring to second guess herself when the sound of a door opening and light footsteps across the hall drew her out of her thoughts. Lucas took a step back as the two women appeared before them, with different looks of surprise on their faces. Anne's was directed at the matching nervous looks the children carried, and Victoria's was a mixture of recognition and confusion at the sight of Eliza.

"You, you are the girl who came here earlier, are you not?" Victoria's voice was as sharp and no-nonsense as it had been earlier the same day, yet to Eliza, it felt like days since they had met.

Eliza could only nod, as she didn't trust her voice to not sound shaky. She felt such joy at seeing the two women, alive and real, that she wanted nothing more than to run up and throw her arms around them; although knowing that they didn't know her had Eliza frozen to the spot, hand holding tight around Lucas' hand. She had only known them for about two nights, but she felt closer to the ghosts, than to any of her friends back home and seeing their hesitancy towards her hurt more than Eliza dared think about.

"Tori, these children, as I've told you, seem to know us from somewhere, and I would very much like to hear their story. Would you care to listen with me, without rushing to judgement?" Although her words were directed to Victoria, Anne kept her eyes on the children and gave them a small reassuring smile.

Victoria pursed her thin lips but gave a curt nod before moving towards the nearest plush couch and sitting down gingerly, muttering something about *lunacy and street children in her house*. Anne extended her hand towards the couch opposite them, asking the children to sit. It took a moment before Eliza moved, tugging Lucas with her. He still seemed frightened. The old couch was like no couch Eliza had sat on before, it was as if she sat upon an inflated balloon instead of a mattress, not giving in to their weight. She gave a slight bounce and found it quite moveable, almost like a trampoline. She bounced some more, delighted in its springs, until the sound of a voice rather loudly stopped her. Victoria looked at her with a raised eyebrow.

"Sorry..." Eliza said sheepishly, shrugging one shoulder.

"Now, tell us your *fascinating* story, child, unless you want to continue your abuse of our couch!" Victoria tutted, earning a slight jab in the ribs by Anne.

"Ah, yes, the story I... Now I know how this will sound."

So, Eliza started to tell her story, starting with her grandparents' house, her meeting the ghosts at night, the rabbit (who she now saw jumping about the room behind Anne), and the portal. Ending with meeting Lucas and then how they ended up in the house.

To say that Anne and Victoria doubted her story would be to putting it mildly. Victoria, whose face had remained in its sharp, stern frown, had loosened into a look of utter bewilderment, with one corner of her lips curled up in half a sneer. Anne's face, whose friendly features could never come across as stern, rounded out. Her mouth hung slightly open, her dark, warm eyes as big as teacups and her thick eyebrows almost disappeared up into her hairline. A soft breath escaped her lips as her eyes shifted between the children. Lucas, who up until that moment had remained silent, shifted in his seat, his eyes glued to the floor as he spoke.

"It's true, well, as much as I know, from the moment we met she has spoken the truth. You learn early on the street when people are lying, and I ain't heard a single thing but the truth from Eliza." He dared to look up and meet Victoria's burning eyes, before quickly continuing.

"Ma'am!" His eyes fell back towards the floor.

A silence filled the room as the occupants contemplated each other. Eliza fidgeted with her hands and her sweater, which now had grown damp and uncomfortable after all the running and slightly rainy weather. She hoped that the women, or Anne at least, believed her and would help her return home. Her eyes drifted from the women to the floor, back to the women, awaiting their reactions.

Lucas sat with his hands folded in his lap, eyes still on the ground, but Eliza could feel him almost vibrate, as if he wanted nothing more than to run for the door. His heart beat so strongly that he was afraid it would soon burst from his chest.

Anne didn't know what to think, or to do. Here were two children, all alone, dirty and one looking injured, saying all these things that defied logic and common sense! Her heart yearned to scoop them up in her arms and soothe their worries, for they both looked so tired and frightened. Yet if there were just a smidgen of truth to their story, they had to do something, yet what that was, she had no idea.

Victoria was filled with conflicting feelings. One part of her wanted to laugh and shoo the children out for daring to come into her house and tell such lies; most likely after money or something, and to yell at Anne for allowing such nonsense to take place! Yet looking at Anne, her darling Anne, and seeing how it affected her, she wanted nothing more than to make her happy, and if that meant going along with this absurd tall tale, then so be it; as long as she was in control of it all. Victoria cleared her throat, getting all their attention before speaking.

"Well, that was quite the story. If we are to believe it, and I'm not saying we are." She put out a hand to silence any rebuttal that Anne was about to cast out.

"It will take a little time to figure out what the next step is to help you, child. So, I suggest we sleep on it and start afresh tomorrow morning. Now, out of the goodness of my friend, and my complacence, I will allow you two to stay the night." Eliza's eyes shot up and found Victoria's, her face lighting up with hope.

"You can stay in the guest room, but the Lord have mercy if I find anything broken or missing come tomorrow!" Her stern voice grew sharp, and Eliza felt rather than saw Lucas shrink down.

"We will behave, I promise!" Eliza said, trying to sound confident and grown up, even though she had never felt as much of a child as she did in that moment.

"Good, now, introduce yourselves properly, then Anne will show you to the room. I want you both at breakfast at seven o'clock, sharp." Victoria stood up as she spoke, keeping her eyes on the children.

They introduced themselves, Eliza even put out her hand for Anne and Victoria to shake. Anne took it gingerly, but Victoria did not. They walked out of the sitting room towards the all too familiar stairs. Eliza was bursting with excitement and nerves. What lay in store for them tomorrow, she didn't know, but the chance of spending more time with her dear ghosts-now alive-before returning home, was more than she could ever have dreamed of. So, with her head held high, the children followed Anne into the next part of their adventure.

Chapter 11
Going Home

Although the house itself was quite grand, it didn't have a lot of rooms, so it came as no surprise to Eliza when she saw which room she and Lucas would sleep in. It was the same bedroom as the one she used when visiting her grandparents. A smile crept up on her lips as her eyes scanned the room. The high ceiling and walls were a light blue colour. The big window across the door stood open, and the smell of the forest after rain filled the bedroom. It surprised Eliza how little her grandparents had changed in the house. However, that was where the similarities ended. A grand, four poster bed stood against the wall; dark and massive, with enough pillows and blankets to make a huge fort out of; she thought, delighted by the possibilities. Beside the bed stood something familiar, but not something Eliza had had in her bedroom. No, this was the large oak wardrobe that was in the attic. Here, though, it looked brand new, and the dark wood almost shone, whereas the one in the attic was dull and bark was missing from the heavy doors. Its brass embellishment looked newly polished, too. Eliza moved towards it, not sure if it was real or just her imagination, for a lot of things had happened, and it was all starting to feel so unreal, as if a pinch or a start would wake her up from this extraordinary dream. When she got close, her hand reached out slowly until her fingers graced the front of the wardrobe. As with the couch downstairs, it too was strange, smooth, intricate and most of all, it was real. Her fingers danced over the wood in gentle motions before the sound of her name being called pulled her attention away. Eliza let her hand fall from the wardrobe as she turned towards Anne.

"Huh?" Eliza looked at the woman quizzically.

"I said, I hope you will be all right sharing the room tonight. The washroom is down the hall, I expect you both to wash before breakfast tomorrow. In the meantime, I will see 'if I can find you both some better clothes in the attic." Anne walked towards the wardrobe, pulled it open and took out two small towels that she placed on the bed.

Eliza's eyebrows knitted together. At the mention of the attic, she was reminded of one thing, or more accurately, one person. She had been so preoccupied by the day; getting lost, meeting Victoria, then Lucas and Anne, seeing them alive, that she hadn't had time to think about who wasn't there with them. How could she have forgotten about Gerald? Sweet, kind Gerald, who had been so interested in her stories and experiences. Before she could think, Eliza started asking…

"Anne, where's Gerald? I haven't seen him at all; is he out of town?"

A shadow fell over Anne's gentle features and her hands, holding on to a slip of her dress, tightened. Her eyes locked on to a point above Eliza's head and she remained as if frozen to the ground for a few minutes. She inhaled sharply and blinked her eyes before meeting Eliza's green ones.

"Oh, sweetheart, I'm afraid you won't be able to meet him. Gerald passed away five months ago."

There was a slight tremor to Anne's voice, as it barely rose above a whisper, but Eliza felt the ice run into her veins and shivered as if the woman had shouted it. Although no tears threatened to fall, Eliza still wiped at her eyes, rubbing them with the back of her still damp sweater.

Anne looked at the girl before taking a step towards her. She wanted to comfort the child, who had no real reason to feel sad about the passing of a man she had never met — unless her story was true, and she knew them, in her own time. No, it was far too much, far too late in the evening. She stopped, hands twining around each other as her eyes wandered over Eliza's features. Shaking her head just a little, Anne turned and walked towards the door, passing by a still shocked Lucas. She gave him a curt nod before talking.

"I will be back with some clothing in a jiff. You just wait here until I get back, then I will show you the washroom before turning in for the night. I suggest you do the same!" And with that, she was out of the door, closing it firmly behind her.

Lucas and Eliza exchanged glances quizzically at the woman's quick departure.

"Was it something I said?" Asked Lucas, smirking.

Eliza laughed. It felt nice to laugh after the day they had had. As Lucas moved towards the window, Eliza looked at the bed. It was massive, and had space for them both, but Eliza had never had someone else in the bed when she slept; not a friend at a sleepover, or even her parents would allow her to share their bed, telling her she kicked and turned too much for them to rest. She glanced over at Lucas who looked to be studying the grounds outside. How she wanted to know what was going on in his head at that moment. All of this was strange enough for her, but he had been dragged into it all, a lone boy with no one else, it seemed; and he was willing to help her get home. Now he was here, in a stranger's house. She wanted to grab his hand and ask him how he felt, but he was miles away. No, they would sleep, and possibly tomorrow it would be easier to ask him, she thought.

A knock sounded, and Anne stepped into the room carrying clothes bundled in her arms. Lucas looked at the woman before walking towards Eliza, grabbing her hand. He was still unsure about it all, and felt immediately safer, knowing she was there.

"Here you are, some undergarments to sleep in, a new shirt for you Lucas, and an old dress that belonged to a niece of mine, Eliza, that I think will fit you." Anne's eyes glided over Eliza's clothes, furrowing her brows. "Such strange clothing, you dress like a boy from the north! Is it customary to wear such in your time?" Anne handed the clothes to the children, meeting Eliza's gaze as she talked.

Eliza shrugged one shoulder, unsure of what to say. "Some of the girls wear trousers, some wear dresses, it depends really. I usually only wear dresses in the summer, and it's too cold now, so I wear wool!" Eliza answered.

Anne gave a hum in response, nodding slightly before continuing. "So, as Victoria said, we shall see you both tomorrow for breakfast. Get some sleep, and if you need anything, our bedroom is at the end of the hall. Pleasant dreams to you both!" and with that, she turned towards the door and started walking away.

Before she reached it, Eliza ran after her and threw her arms around the woman's waist, giving her a tight squeeze and muttering a silent thank you. Eliza released her and took a step back, cheeks red. Anne looked at the girl, slightly startled, but gave a small smile before bidding them good night and walking out.

The children undressed and put on the garments they were given. They were both too big but it didn't bother them. As they climbed into the bed, they tried not to look at each other. Lucas held his gaze firmly on the ceiling above as Eliza's eyes flitted across the room. Neither wanting to sleep, yet the day had been long, and fatigue clung to them both. Lucas could feel his eyelids drooping, yet he fought to keep them open. Eliza looked at him then, seeing his struggle to stay awake.

"Are you all right?" she asked.

and…

Eliza wanted to say something, wanted to reassure him that he was safe with her, but she knew it wouldn't help, for he must be too scared to trust a girl he had just met. She took a deep breath before turning towards him in the bed.

"When I get scared, I sing a lullaby my father used to sing to me when I was little. Do you want me to sing it to you?" She tried to sound calming, but the tears had clogged her throat, and the words came out too rough. Lucas gave a shrug, as if it didn't matter to him what she did. So, Eliza made herself comfortable, lying next to the boy and started to sing.

"My dear, my dear, it's time to sleep. Close your eyes now and breathe and breathe for me. The day has been so long, so long, so long. And my dear, it's time to sleep. In your dreams you'll sing and dance and play and do all that you dare not say. For there you are free, as free as you can be. And my dear it's time to sleep."

Lucas' eyes had closed, Eliza noticed. Her hand moved to brush a strand of hair from his forehead, and he let out a sigh, sinking deeper into the pillow beneath him. She continued stroking his forehead as she remembered her mother doing it to her.

"My dear, my dear, it's time to sleep. When you wake up you'll see, you'll see. That you are all you dared to be. My dear it's time to sleep. You are free, as free as a deer, you sing like a bird. You dance like the wind, like the wind, my dear, and you play like the sea. But for now, my dear, it's time to sleep, so sleep, my dear, so sleep."

The steady rise and fall of his chest told Eliza that he had fallen asleep. She stopped stroking his forehead and placed her hand next to the sleeping boy. Her own lullaby still going in her head, the words tugging at her heart and the sound lulling away her worries. Before she knew it, she too was pulled into dreamland.

***

Victoria sat down in the kitchen chair besides Anne with a heavy sigh, a lit cigarette hanging from between her lips. She moved a slightly shaken hand through her hair before looking at the other woman. Anne had had a worried look in her eyes since she had sent the children to bed but had yet to say anything about it. Victoria took a deep drag of the cigarette before settling it between her fingers on the table.

"Are you going to tell me what happened upstairs?" She tried to keep her voice light, although she felt anything but concern.

Anne looked at her as if only now feeling her presence and gave her a small smile that didn't reach her eyes. They had known each other for many years, since childhood, and they had stayed close all through Victoria's marriage to Gerald. It had been Anne who had been her bridesmaid at the wedding. It had been Anne who helped her with the garden, the parties and the lonely days when Gerald's work had taken up so much of his time that he had barely been home for as long as a week. It had been Anne who held her and comforted her when Gerald had passed away, and it had been Anne who had moved in when the house had been too empty and big.

Victoria would do anything for her friend if asked, or even if not asked, but what her friend had brought into her house that night was taking its toll on the older woman, and she feared it would be too much even for them to handle. So, when Anne only looked at her, with her warm eyes and kind smile, it almost broke her heart to see the tears start to fall from those eyes.

Subconsciously, Victoria turned the old ring on her right wedding finger, around and around. It was an old habit with an even older ring her grandmother had given her. It was a heavy glass eye with what looked to be tree branches circled around as the iris; and when she felt herself getting anxious, agitated or upset, she would turn the ring around and around on her finger. Anne's shaky breath drew her out from her thoughts.

"I'm not sure what to say, really. Yet I get the feeling that the little girl is telling the truth, and I must admit that it frightens me. Tori, what are we going to do?" Anne finally asked.

Victoria looked down at her hands; looked at the cigarette that had now burned down to ash, looked at the old ring with the light blue eye looking back at her, before slowly shaking her head.

"Dear Anne, what have you brought into our lives?"

***

Eliza woke with a start. Her heart felt as if it was beating its way out of her chest and she didn't know where she was. A clock chimed somewhere in the house and a cold wind blew through the half-opened window. Everything was dark, so it must still be night time, she thought. Movement to her left told her she wasn't alone, and she almost shrieked in surprise. She could just make out the figure of a boy. Then it came back to her; where she was, what had happened and who was next to her. The chiming from the clock still sounded as she leaned over and shook Lucas.

"Lucas, Lucas!" A half muffled growl came from the boy as he moved. Eliza shook him again and he shot up, awake and confused.

"What's that!" His voice was all sleep.

"Don't be so loud! I just wanted to see if you were there." The girl's comment made him give a huff before falling back onto the bed.

"You woke me up just to see if I was still here?" He didn't look at her. His right hand rubbed at his eyes as he turned away from her.

Eliza was flustered. Not knowing what to say, she shoved his shoulder. He sat up again, fixing her with an indignant look.

"What's the matter with you? I just fell asleep!"

Eliza huffed. She didn't want to tell him that she'd had a nightmare, not when he was acting like that, anyway. The sound of creaking wood and light footsteps froze them both.

"D-did you hear that?" Eliza asked.

Lucas said nothing. He found Eliza's hand and held it tight.

Seconds past until déjà vu hit Eliza. She remembered a night not long ago with a similar sound, and an idea shot up. Hope grew in her chest at the thought. Although the women in the house were alive, one of her friends was not. What if, she wondered, what if there was a ghost here already? She jumped out of the bed and scrambled towards the wardrobe, pulling it open.

"What in the Good Heavens are you doing?" Lucas asked as he got out of the bed.

"I'll explain! First, I need to find a robe or something to wear." Eliza pulled out some bed sheets before exclaiming, "Aha!" Pulling out two robes she threw one to Lucas before putting on the other and tying it around her waist.

"You remember I told you how I knew the people who live here?"

Lucas nodded in the dark and gave a hum.

"They were ghosts! And when I saw they were alive, I forgot about it, but then Anne told us that Gerald was gone. What if he isn't?" Eliza walked up to the boy, placing her hands on his shoulders.

"You lost me there…" Eliza tugged at him as she pointed to the door.

"I think Gerald is here, not as a human, but as a ghost! We should go up to the attic and see if we can find him!"

"Are you mental?" Lucas stood frozen to the ground, unwilling to move.

Eliza rolled her eyes as she moved towards the boy, grabbing his hand and tugging him towards the door.

"No need to be scared, Lucas, he's just a ghost!"

Eliza took great care not to make much noise as they left the bedroom. Even if she could move to the staircase blindfolded without a creak sounding, she knew Lucas couldn't, so their hands stayed linked as she manoeuvred them across the hallway. The hall was submerged in darkness as the only window had thick curtains hanging over them. Obscuring the only light source they tiptoed forwards, ears pricked for any noise either from the attic or the other bedroom. Then a soft *clank* sound from upstairs.

"What was that!" Lucas asked, his voice several octaves higher than usual.

Eliza shushed him as they continued to walk. When they reached the stairs, Eliza turned to look at Lucas. She tried to find his bright eyes in the darkness before speaking.

"Okay, when you meet Gerald, let me do the talking, got it? Try not to scream, it won't do us any good if you wake up the entire house and we get kicked out on our arses!" Eliza held his gaze. Lucas could barely make her eyes out in the dark, but he could swear her eyes burned with a fire he had never seen before.

He nodded, not trusting his voice to carry. Slowly, they walked up the stairs, soft creaks and groans from the floorboards making them stop to check if they had been heard. Soon enough they were standing outside the door to the attic. Eliza could feel Lucas shaking but gave it no thought. She told him to be brave, and to remember not to scream, then she opened the door.

The attic that belonged to Victoria and Anne was much more clean and less cluttered than the one belonging to her grandparents, Eliza saw. The furniture and artefacts spread around the room seemed to be unused or simply waiting. Nothing was broken as far as she could see, and the cobwebs and dust were almost not visible. Yet that was all there was in the attic, furniture and cobwebs; no ghosts or tea sets. Eliza walked into the room and turned in all directions, looking. Lucas walked behind her, closing the door before standing beside his friend.

"Hello, is there anyone here? Gerald?" Eliza asked the empty room.

There was a soft ruffling of sheets, then the creaking of an opening door, and a gasp sounded from Lucas as a shadow appeared underneath the window in the roof. A misty grey figure moved towards them, and then what could possibly have been a man stood before them. Eliza took a step forward and was about to say something when a scream pierced the silence. She turned around just in time to see Lucas backing away right into a low ceiling beam, fear evident on his face. He fell onto the floor.

***

A low groan sounded from the boy on the floor. His head ached and his heart beat wildly as a wild animal trying to tear its way out of his chest. The attic floor was bone-chillingly cold beneath him and seeped through his thin nightgown. His hand reached up to touch his forehead and his eyes fluttered open. As his eyes focused, he could see two shapes leaning above him. One he knew as his friend, her nightshirt hanging off her body and her curly hair standing out in angles and falling like a curtain over her round face. The other figure was a mystery. Greyish features made out the man — was it a man at his friend's side? With stubble on his face, a top hat in his hands and bright, inquisitive eyes peering down on him, he looked like any normal old man. Yet, Lucas knew he wasn't just a man, he was a ghost, for all of him was grey, like the man was made from city fog. Lucas wondered if a breeze would be able to take him away from them. He looked back at Eliza and noticed that she had been speaking. Another groan escaped him. Lucas could swear he saw worry in the old man's eyes. Fear still flowed through his body, but he felt no need to scream again; not that he would ever have acknowledged screaming again if anyone had asked.

"Lucas, are you okay?" said Eliza.

"You gave us quite the fright, young man!" That must be the old man, Lucas thought.

He tried to sit up, although his muscles ached from the movement. A hand reached out and he grabbed it as he stood up. The room started to spin, and he leaned on Eliza to steady himself. Lucas looked at his friend and gave a pained smile. The look he received could only be described as a mother looking at her child who had hurt themself doing something they were told not to do. He could do nothing but look sheepishly at her.

"So, child, now that your friend is up and well, will you please explain to me what you are doing in my attic?" The old man had floated, yes floated, away from the children, and was looking at them with a questioning glance.

Lucas looked from the man, to Eliza, then back at the man. The girl wasted no time in telling her story for the second time that evening, and as she spoke, he kept a close watch on the old man. He didn't seem mean, or cruel, or upset. His clothes looked to be well made and his eyes sparkled, even though they were grey they could never be dull. As Eliza spoke, his face morphed from curious, to confused, to delighted.

"My, that is quite the story, little girl. Am I to believe it? My logical mind is telling me no, yet the knowledge that I am no longer alive gives it a bit of truth that I hardly can refute. As for you being from the future, you said, it's hard to fathom. To travel through time is simply a notion of fiction." Eliza's face fell into a look of absolute defeat at the man's words.

"However, as you are standing here in front of me, calling me by my name and telling me my stories, I find my faith wavering. For we have never met before, I certainly would have remembered, yet you speak to me as a dear friend. I am a gentleman and one who prides himself in generosity and comradery, I never turn away a friend, especially one in need!" His deep voice was no-nonsense, yet as he spoke, a mischievous smile spread across his face.

Eliza's head shot up and a squeal that nearly pierced Lucas' ears erupted from her. The girl rolled on her feet back and forth, seemingly trying to stop herself from running up to the man. Lucas couldn't help but smile at Eliza's antics. The girl was a strange one. One moment she would be burning with emotion, needing to move, to touch, to grab to jump around, as if the emotions were firing her up, and standing still was as impossible as walking on water. Then, she could be as cold as ice, frozen to the ground, as untouchable as the wind around them and so far away in her head, he presumed, that not even a cannon blast could bring her out of it. He knew if she had held his hand in that moment, she would have held it so tightly it would have turned blue.

"I have so many questions!" Eliza said, moving again towards the man.

The night Lucas saw his first ghost was a night he would remember, and cherish, as long as he lived. Eliza had asked as many questions as she had breaths in her lungs, and Gerald, the old man, had answered them all in his warm and gentle voice before asking his own. They had talked for what seemed like hours. Lucas told about what was happening in the world; about politics, about the new ferry in east London, about the new tower built and opened in Paris and about his own adventures around the city. They had laughed, shared stories and even danced a little, Eliza had insisted for some strange reason that they played the gramophone but no such thing was to be found in the attic, so they danced without music. Then, as they had finally calmed down from their dance, the chime of a clock could be heard throughout the house. Eliza stood up before giving a small bow that earned her a few laughs from the others, before Gerald gave them a grandfatherly look and told them to hop down to bed.

Lucas extended his hand to say farewell. Gerald laughed deeply, as only an old man could, and Eliza snickered. Lucas could feel his ears turning a deep red as realisation dawned on him, and he hurriedly put his hand down before giving a light punch to Eliza's shoulder. She returned the punch before turning back to the old man. Her goodbye died on her lips as she found the space where the man had stood empty. The children exchanged glances.

"Well, that was odd…" Lucas finally said.

"More odd than talking to a ghost?" Eliza asked, a knowing smirk on her lips.

Lucas gave a huff and rolled his eyes before walking out of the room with Eliza right on his heels, peals of laughter followed the two out the door.

***

A knock on the door was the first thing Eliza heard when she woke up. Tangled in sheets and limbs, almost unable to move, her head shot up from the pillow it had been resting on. The bedroom was cold, too cold for the girl as a shiver ran down her body. She looked to her side and found a deeply sleeping, slightly snoring boy. One arm draped over his eyes, the other clenched around a piece of Eliza's nightgown, his left leg fully on top of the cover, while the other was hooked around her own leg. A twinge of sadness tugged at her heart at the sight. She herself was halfway out of the bed, the cover over just the leg tangled with Lucas'. No wonder she felt cold. She wondered if the boy had held on to her by choice as they fell asleep last night, or if his mind needed to feel that he wasn't alone, and when he had been reassured that she was there, he was unwilling to let go in case she disappeared. The knock sounded again, pulling Eliza from her thoughts, turning her head towards the door. It opened to reveal a smiling and fully composed Anne.

"Good morning children. Breakfast will be ready soon; time to get up and get ready for the day!" Her voice was as bright and bubbly as ever and it immediately calmed Eliza.

"Good morning to you too Anne, we'll be down soon!" Eliza's voice was filled with sleep, and the words barely sounded as words when she spoke. Anne gave a nod before reminding her not to be late, then she closed the door. Eliza could hear her footsteps receding down the hall.

She let her head fall back down onto the pillow as she gave a heavy sigh. After breakfast she was going to go home. She needed to get back, but every fibre in her body screamed at her to stay, to be with her new friends, to stay with Lucas, for what would happen to him when she left? Would he return to the streets and be one more of the lost children? Not if she could prevent it.

Eliza looked at the boy. If she could, she would take him with her. Her parents would understand, right? They would help him find a family and they would be together forever! If he wanted to come with her, of course that would be okay. Her brows furrowed as she thought about it, but the start of a headache made her sit up. Now was not the time, they had to get dressed and go down for breakfast.

"Hey, Hey, Lucas, wake up!" Eliza pushed at the boy's shoulder as she spoke. A mumble of words and a groan was all she got in reply.

She rolled her eyes before shoving harder. Still no reply. As a final act, Eliza reached behind her, picked up her pillow and smacked the boy square in the face. Lucas shot up, arms waving about, his head swinging back and forth to see what had happened. When they landed on the laughing girl who was doing everything not to fall off the bed, arms wrapped around her stomach as she rocked back and forth with laughter, he gave her a dirty look before throwing the pillow full force back into her face. The pillow hit with such force that Eliza fell back off the bed as she shrieked, arms flailing about.

It was Lucas's time to laugh at the sight of Eliza on the floor; hair, nightgown and limbs all over the place. He stopped laughing though when the girl got up, fuming so much that he feared steam would come out of her ears. With the pillow in hand, Eliza let out a warrior's cry before pouncing on the boy. It was an all-out war then, pillows, covers and feathers flying with wild abandon as shrieks, laughter and thuds sounded. Eliza swore she would have a few bruises tomorrow but she didn't care. She hadn't had that much fun in ages. When they ended the fight (Lucas said he had won, Eliza strongly disagreed), they were lying in opposite directions on the bed, chests heaving and giggles floating out between breaths. Eliza felt as if she was forgetting something.

She gasped as she shot up and whispered a word she was explicitly not allowed to use, ever. She yelled at Lucas to hurry up and get dressed before frantically searching for her new clothes. When she finally found them, her eyes grew as big as saucers. What in the world was she looking at? There were cloths of what looked like cotton, some white, some in a creamy looking colour and a final two piece one in a light blue. The blue one was the thickest of all the clothes and seemed like the right one to put on. Then there were long socks that reached up over her knees and ribbons. Eliza didn't know what to do with half of the items, and a glance at Lucas told her he didn't know either. Whereas he got a new, albeit a little big, shirt and what looked like suspenders her dad would wear at Christmas. Lucas was almost the same and was dressed within minutes. Eliza sighed as she draped the skirt half around her nightgown and put on the top half like a jacket. It had so many buttons that Eliza lost count on how many she did-up that she skipped at least half a dozen before putting on the too long socks. She felt silly in her getup and worried, thinking she had done something wrong. Too afraid of being late, she pushed the thought to the back of her head. No need to worry too much. She stepped towards the door and pulled on her old rain boots, as she didn't have any other shoes. They made her feel more comfortable and she was thankful for them, nonetheless. Eliza left her hair a wild mass of curls, feeling no need to fix it. Lucas stepped up behind her and together they walked out and down the stairs.

The clatter of feet running at breakneck speed was the only warning the two women sitting in the well-lit kitchen were given before two bushy haired children stood breathing heavily in the doorway. They exchanged puzzled glances, as neither of them were used to having children around. The newcomers were talking, voices high and light, as they moved towards them. Anne couldn't fight her smile as she looked at them. Their joy was contagious and it had been a while since such happiness had filled the house. Victoria, on the other hand, disapproved. Her pursed lips and pinched eyebrows made her look centuries older than she was, and Anne wondered if she would suffer permanent damage to her features if her face stayed like that for much longer. Eliza stopped moving when she saw Victoria's expression, tugging Lucas behind her.

"Good morning!" Eliza gave a lopsided smile, her voice slightly wavering.

Victoria gave a sniff while Anne restrained herself from sending a well-aimed elbow into her friends midriff. She, on the other hand, smiled at the two figures before her.

"Good morning to you both, I hope you slept well!" Anne got up from where she had been sitting and moved around the table towards the children. Now that she gave them a closer look, she stopped suddenly, mouth open.

"My dear girl, what, or more appropriately *how*, are you wearing?"

Eliza looked down at herself with a frown. Her gown was a little crooked, all right, and maybe she had forgotten a button or two *or twelve*, but she was dressed wasn't she? It wasn't her fault that the clothes were so difficult to put on. Why she couldn't have gotten a shirt like Lucas, she didn't know. She crossed her arms, both in slight defiance and to cover herself up. Anne took two steps closer before bending down in front of the girl, hands reaching out and ready to pull at the gown. Eliza took a step back, unease making her pull her shoulders up around her ears. Anne pulled back her hands before asking Eliza if she could help her correct the garment. The girl gave a nod as the older woman started to fix her buttons, tugged at it and pulled up the stockings that almost slipped down completely to her feet. When she was pleased with her work, Anne gave a squeeze to Eliza's arm before righting herself and turning towards Lucas. His eyes flickered to Eliza and then back to Anne. She just gave him a wink.

"You managed to dress very well, dear!" Lucas pushed out his chest at the compliment and Eliza couldn't help but snicker at her friends. In turn, he put out his tongue at her.

"Now, Anne, that the children are presentable, can we please eat?" Victoria's voice was airy, but one could hear the exasperation laced within. Anne just rolled her eyes at the children as she spoke in the sweetest voice Eliza had heard her use.

"Why of course, my dearest Tori, we fly on the swift wings of angels to your side, lest hunger takes you away from us!" As she spoke, Anne lifted her arms out to her sides, flapping her hands up and down gently as she moved towards Victoria.

Eliza and Lucas couldn't hold in their laughter at the woman's antics. They followed her, not flapping their arms though, and sat down on the remaining chairs around the table. Eliza was surprised at the generous spread the table held. There were fruits cut in bowls, fresh bread already cut into slices and meats and cheeses that smelt heavenly.

Her stomach growled at the sight and she had to fight the blush threatening to creep up her neck. Lucas seemed just as overwhelmed as Eliza. She had a nagging thought that this was possibly the first time he had seen so much food in one place that he was allowed to eat. At Anne's request, they started eating. The food tasted as heavenly as it looked. Although Eliza could be a picky eater, the knowledge that she hadn't eaten since breakfast yesterday morning made her throw caution to the wind. It felt like such a long time ago, yesterday; sitting with her grandparents in the same house, in the very room she was in now. Only yesterday was centuries away, yet only a mere 24-hours gone.

The conversations around the table were light, talking about nothing and everything from the weather, to gardening, to what they would be having for tea. Eliza tagged along, asking and answering between mouthfuls, trying to remember her table manners as best she could. The reproachful look she got from Victoria when she had started talking about football, with juice from an apple running down her chin, made her cheeks burn as she hurried to swab at the liquid with the sleeve of her gown. That had obviously been the wrong thing to do as Victoria let out a huff before leaning over and dabbing a napkin at Eliza's face. The gesture warmed the young girl's heart making her feel embarrassed. It was strange how the older woman could be so caring and yet so resentful, as if every act of kindness hurt her gravely.

Eliza didn't really know where to place the woman. Yes, she was resentful, short-tempered and looked like everyone around her was beneath her, but she had let two unknown children come into her home and she was willing to help them at the behest of her friend. Eliza knew her as she remembered the care and warmth she had seen in the woman's eyes when they had first met. It was as if she were two different persons. Just thinking about it made a headache start to bloom behind the girl's eyes. What would it take to change this Victoria into the ghost she knew?

As the breakfast ended and the conversations stilled, a strange silence filled the room. Anne's eyes flitted to and fro around the table. Eliza fixed her eyes squarely on the plate in front of her, Lucas started a staring contest with one of the fruits untouched at the table, his leg bouncing in a quick rhythm under it. Victoria, whose eyes had been on Anne the whole time, glanced up at the clock hanging near the door.

"Well, this has been a lovely morning and a beautiful breakfast. Yet, the hour is late, and we both have business to take care of today." At the pause, Victoria looked to Anne again; "and we mustn't be late. Let's get the girl home, then we can see to the boy."

Eliza's eyes shot up to Victoria. Lucas's leg stopped its bouncing as his eyes went to Anne, a nervous look etched on his face.

"Is it really time to go already?" The words fell from Eliza's lips before she had a chance to stop herself. She wanted to go home, didn't she? Of course she would miss Lucas, and it would be strange to go back to the ghosts in the attic, her grandparents and even her parents who would be waiting. They were probably searching for her, and they would be angry, thinking she had run away or something. No, in that moment, Eliza didn't want to go.

As if Anne had read her mind, she placed a hand on Eliza's shoulder, saying how lovely it had been to meet her, but that it was time to go home where she belonged and where her family would be waiting. Eliza wanted to say that they were her family too, but knew they wouldn't understand, as grownups usually didn't understand the minds of children. That she had received more care and warmth from the two women sitting at either side of her at the table than from her parents was not something to blurt out.

Her parents were usually busy with work and didn't have as much time for the girl as she would like. In some ways she understood. They had explained to her multiple times that what they did was important, and for them to live happily, they had to work like they did. Eliza didn't care how they lived, as long as they made time to spend with her; showed that they were interested in her and spent time together as a family. Eliza blinked her eyes, trying to stop the tears from falling as she nodded her head. It was time to go.

***

The cool morning air hit Eliza's face and she shuddered. Her gown did little to stop the wind from seeping into her bones and the clothes she had worn yesterday were left behind, too dirty and ruined to wear, as Victoria had said. The earth had frozen solid during the night, leaving behind wizened flowers and dried leaves rustling across the ground. The entire garden looked to have aged years in the hours the night had brought, as if the dark had stolen the very life out of the earth. The figures moving across the garden were as different in stature as in their feelings about the parting that was to take place.

Eliza, half hidden behind Victoria's tall frame, walked with as short a step as she could without falling too far behind, her mind battling with itself. While she wanted to go home, she loathed herself for wanting to stay. She was surrounded by new friends, people she knew cared about her, or would care in the future. At home waited the monotony of everyday life, with family who didn't notice her, a school she didn't like and a life with no excitement.

To some extent, she knew it wasn't fair to think like that, but to her young mind everything that happened in the moment carried more weight than what had been. The conflict she felt within made her stomach turn and the pain made her want to cry even more.

Lucas walked beside the girl, hands clasped firmly together in a last show of friendship. Although he was sad to lose his new friend, he knew that her going home was the right thing. She would be with family, in her own time, and she would be happy there. That was all he cared about, he thought. He tried to ignore the anger he felt at her leaving. It was not his place to be angry at his friend for leaving, just because she was going home and he would be going back out onto the street where once again he had to fight for food with the other orphans and homeless children. No, he would swallow his feelings and wish Eliza nothing more than reassurance and happiness.

Victoria, leading the strange group, had feelings she did not wish to feel. Once the girl was home, it would all be over and things would return to normal. Though the nagging feeling of unease crept up her spine, she walked with her head held high. Her mind seemed to have other ideas. The boy, for he was just that; a young boy, maybe twelve or thirteen; what would happen to him? From what the girl had told them, he was homeless or an orphan, she couldn't recall, and would disappear from them now, but to go where? There were a lot of children living on the streets. One couldn't travel anywhere in London without seeing one, and it had always upset her. Most were filthy little things, running around, stealing and causing trouble, and most of the time she looked away. Yet she felt her heart break for the little ones. When she had been married to Gerald, they had tried but never conceived a child. Victoria never minded that too much, but she knew Gerald had always wanted children, and to not be able to give her loving husband one tore at her pride.

One day they had been walking during winter, and a blizzard had started up, tearing at their frocks and nipping at their necks. As they walked, they had spotted two children huddled under a wagon, shivering. Gerald had walked over to them, and without saying a word gave them his outer coat. He had almost passed away from a cold after that. His unyielding care broke something in her. So, every winter thereafter, without saying anything to her husband or dearest friend, she had ordered extra yarn and knitted as many small sweaters as her fingers could muster, careful not to spill any blood when her fingers had cracked, before walking the streets early on winter mornings and handing them out to as many children as she met. Casting a glance over at the boy, she saw him as one of the children she had passed during her walks and suppressed a shiver. No, he would not be one of them this winter.

Walking next to her was Anne, a few steps behind, tugging at the hem of her overcoat. It was all so strange, she thought. It had been a normal day, and now, not even twenty-four hours later, everything had changed. Two children had entered hers and Tori's lives and told them things not even dreamed of in fiction, and now they were saying goodbye forever. With a heart that could fit the world, as Victoria had once told her, the children had found their place in it, and she was reluctant to watch them go. The girl would go home, off to the future, if you could believe it, and be safely returned to her awaiting family. She was such a sweet girl; clever and talkative, caring and brave, things Anne wished all little girls could be. Yet the world around them cared not for such girls and did its damndest to make them fit into what they felt girls should do, act and be. She had had to change when she grew up, as her overly kind heart and too free mind didn't fit with what her family and society felt she should be. It had caused her many years of unease and discomfort. It wasn't until she had met Victoria and Gerald that she had felt free enough to be herself, and after all the years of trying to be what everyone else wanted her to be, it took some time for her to find herself again; but they had stayed with her through it all, had encouraged her and loved her unconditionally to the point where she felt no fear or embarrassment over being whoever she truly was. Anne felt forever in her dear friend's debt. Now, however, was no time to walk down memory lane. She turned her head and gave a warm smile to the two children behind her.

"Eliza, would you care to take the lead?" Anne asked.

The girl's head shot up to meet her gaze. She too had seemed lost inside her mind. Eliza gave a nod as she walked up beside the woman, tentatively reaching up and clasping their hands together. The act startled Anne but she didn't pull away.

The walk through the garden and subsequent woods turned out to be slightly more difficult than either of the women thought it would be. As they watched Eliza and Lucas duck, jump and even climb their way through the woods, they struggled to keep up. Neither one of them was young any more, and it had been ages since they both had walked in such terrain without a path. After a big old twig snapped off in Victoria's perfectly prim updo -Victoria had yelped at the sensation, frozen to the spot, causing Anne to not so gently crash into her back. Lucas had lost his footing coming down from a particularly tall branch and made Eliza jump, turn and stare at her three companions. The older woman let out an incredibly loud and exasperated sigh.

"Now, I am not one to sound like a petulant little child, but are we *there* yet?" Victoria asked, sounding very much like a child.

Eliza looked around. It wasn't easy finding her way back, she had, after all, been following a rabbit the first time she had ended up there, and her walk back had been laced with confusion and bewilderment. She spotted what she assumed was a tree that looked familiar and pointed.

"Yes, we are getting close, I think it's just behind that tree!" She resumed walking after lending a hand to Lucas, whose bottom had impacted with the frozen ground.

The trees surrounding them stood tall and thick, and Eliza found herself leaning on one as she looked around. She was quite certain they were close. A few more steps, over that bush, through that small clearing, and there she would see the same moss laden rocks and the great pine. She could hear the procession walking behind her as she continued, guiding them as best she could. Eliza picked up her speed, knowing how close they were, sure that they would be able to see her as she moved ahead.

She needed to be sure she was right, and if not, she could rack her brains about the location before they could ask more questions. She went over the bush, through the clearing and there, she could see the pine! Eliza felt confident and turned her head to shout out to the others as she neared it. Yet when she looked back, all traces of confidence disappeared, and confusion took its place. Her eyes scanned everything ahead of her. Every rock, tree, bush and pinecone, it was all there, as she remembered. The heavy breathing behind her told her the group had caught up. Someone touched her shoulder, Lucas most likely.

"Why have you stopped, Eliza?" Lucas asked between breaths.

Eliza didn't answer at first, her eyes still flitting around. Her chest screamed, and she drew out a breath, unsure of how long she had held it. She could feel her knees starting to give out and she wanted nothing more than to fall to the ground. Instead she turned to the boy.

"T-the portal. It isn't here! It should be there, right by that pine tree and those rocks, but it's not there, Lucas. It's not there!"

Chapter 12
The Owl and the Rabbit

The only sound to be heard in the woods was the wind howling gently amongst the trees. No one dared breathe or speak as Eliza's words hit them. The girl, shivering with what could either have been fear or confusion, fell to her knees before the large tree. Her hands frantically searching the ground around her. The touch of a hand on her shoulder drew her back as she sat down fully. Tears ran freely down her cheek and Eliza made no move to remove them. Then Lucas, who's hand she realised had been the one on her shoulder, emerged within eyesight. He looked about to speak when a loud *huff!* came from behind them.

"So, you're telling us it's *not* here? Are you quite certain? For as it looks now, I am starting to believe that you fabricated this whole story up for — for some childish need for attention!" Victoria shouted.

A sharp *shush* and *Tori, really?* from Anne.

Eliza could feel something breaking on the inside of her chest at the words, and something else hardening. She shook her head, slowly, before turning to look at

Lucas. He, in turn, crouched beside her, staring daggers at Victoria, before mumbling reassurance to the girl.

"Don't listen to her, Eliza, I know you're not lying!" He told her in hushed tones.

Then another pair of hands touched the back of her neck. Anne's calm voice sounded just behind her.

"Eliza, dear, are you certain you haven't just taken a wrong turn? We will come searching with you if you still want us to." Anne, too, sent a rather reproachful look to her friend.

"Oh honestly, Anne, we don't have time for this. I have a meeting that I *cannot* be late to. This has gone on long enough! I- I am not happy that we cannot be of more help, truthfully. However, I see no need to support this foolish course any longer!" For a usually composed and put together woman, Victoria looked and sounded to Eliza like someone on the brink of a slight meltdown.

No, Eliza was sure. This was the place the portal should be, but no longer was. She took Lucas' outstretched hand as he pulled her upright. Her legs felt unstable as she moved away from where she had landed, her gaze fixed on the oldest of the group. Her eyes narrowed as courage flared in her chest.

"I *know* this is where it should be, and I am NOT lying! There is no need to look elsewhere, but if we were to…" Eliza had to fight to get the words out around the lump that had lodged itself in her throat. "I wouldn't want *you* with us!" She spat the last words at the woman before turning on her heel and walking towards Anne and Lucas, who stood huddled together.

Victoria's jaw twitched as she pressed her teeth together, eyes following the retreating child. She turned her chin slightly upwards haughtily, returning to her usual dignified posture, before finding her friend's unreadable face. She raised both her eyebrows in an exasperated question, and when she received no answer, huffed and crossed her arms over her chest before uncrossing them again.

Anne looked mournful then, sighing before tentatively reaching out and placing her hand on Eliza's shoulder, eyes turning towards the girl. Murmuring words of comfort and reassurance, the shorter brunette looked at the children next to her before saying loud enough for Victoria to hear:.

"As Victoria said..." Victoria blanched slightly at the coldness her name had been said with. "We have some business to attend to today, but I would not feel comfortable leaving you two alone in the house; nor I'm sure our butler Mr Holden would agree or God forbid, out on the street in this weather. So, I think it would be best that you accompany Victoria and me. After our meetings, perhaps we could meet up and go over what to do next; perhaps for lunch?" Eliza's anger melted away as happiness overcame her, eyes locking with Lucas', whose eyes showed the same excitement she felt.

Victoria, who had taken several steps closer, cleared her inexplicably dry throat and was about to ask whether she had a say in this at all, but was stopped rather firmly by her companions' sharp gaze. She gave a sniff, a slight curl of her lip, but inclined her head in a short nod. She knew better than to argue with her dearest friend when Anne looked at her like that.

Victoria did not give way to others, especially when they were out of bounds. The socialising and gatherings she had hosted and taken part-in had always, in some way or another, worked to her advantage. Whenever a housewife or an old friend had started debating or the gossip had turned sour, Victoria would turn the conversations in her favour, and she had never let anyone's opinions sway her. Because of the headstrong upbringing she'd had, there were few people who could — or even dared to oppose her, except for Anne. Victoria had learnt early on that the younger woman was not to be trifled with when she had made up her mind, and despite her cheery disposition; there was an unrelenting stubbornness in her that could grow like mould on walls and render whole friendships crumbling to the floor with merely a few words.

Anne gave her a warm smile now that she had gotten her way, taking each child by the hand as they made their way back towards the house, at a slightly more relaxed pace. With a sigh that threatened to shake her very foundation, Victoria picked up her feet and followed the retreating bodies.

Eliza let her mind go blank. She willed it to stay silent,; yet the crushing weight of all that had transpired within the last few hours slowly ate away at the back of her mind. It was all too much; too many feelings, too many conflicting thoughts running rampant. She just wanted to enjoy the knowledge that she would get to spend time with her new friends, more time with the boy who had, in such a short time, come to mean the world to her. The woman whose warm hand she held, brought a level of safety to her that she had never experienced before. She squared her shoulders and walked along, letting the small conversation between Anne and Lucas flow unhindered.

Eliza could hear the slow footfalls of Victoria behind them but she decided not to pay any attention to the woman. She could stay behind them in silence for all she cared. The older woman's anger confused and hurt the girl, and she wanted nothing more at that moment than to be far away from her. She had thought that Victoria would have been more understanding, that the icy front that she had met them with had melted away after breakfast, but it seemed that the cold woman had a heart to match. It was a childish thing, really, but as with most children, hope lay closer to the surface, and Eliza had seen the gentleness and warmth the woman was capable of, and that small glimmer of empathy, had allowed her to hold onto her belief that Victoria could and would change. She decided then, that no matter how distant and icy the woman was, she would melt her, mould her into the ghost she could become, no matter what. Eliza was brought out of her scheming thoughts by Anne tugging gently on her hand. They had stopped moving.

"What do you think, Eliza? Would you be okay with going together with Lucas and Victoria? Where I'm going, it would not do to bring children along, especially children I would seem out of bounds with," Anne asked, eyes questioning as they held Eliza's.

Although Eliza didn't understand all of what the woman had said, Anne's voice gave little room for disagreement, and as loath as she would be to go anywhere with Victoria at that moment, she wanted to show Anne how thankful she was for the woman's kindness. And if that meant going along with her plans, she would do so gladly, or as close to gladly as she could come at that moment. She swallowed the remains of the lump in her throat and nodded.

"A… all right, where would we be going?" Eliza hadn't heard Victoria coming up beside them and was startled when her clear voice answered.

"As I said earlier, I have an important meeting in the city."

She raised a hand to stop Eliza from asking anything, as she had seen the girl starting to talk. Eliza furrowed her brows in a glare at the action.

"It is of no concern of yours what the meeting is about, child. We will return to the house to put on more decent winter coats as the weather is not easing up, and then we will take a carriage into the city. I expect you both to be at your best behaviour, and to keep silent in the presence of others!" Ice had seeped from Victoria's face into her voice, causing a shudder to run down Eliza's back. The glare stayed as the woman spoke, but she gave a nod in understanding.

Lucas, who had remained silent during the conversation piped up. "Are we going to stay by your side all the time?" He visibly shrank back when Victoria turned her stare towards him.

"It would be prudent to have you close for most of the journey. However, I will be conducting the meeting alone. You will stay wherever I tell you to stay." The boy nodded quickly, eager to get the woman's ire onto someone else.

Victoria gave a humph in response before turning around and walking the short distance back towards the house. When she was out of earshot, both Anne and Lucas let out a breath at the same time. It would have been comical if not for the tension clearly visible on Anne's shoulders. Shaking herself to get rid of the tension, Anne reached out her hands towards the children who in turn each took a hand as they started walking again. After a few feet, Lucas leaned slightly back from Anne, found Eliza's gaze before widening his eyes and made a grimace with his face; a look that made Eliza try, and fail, to suppress a giggle.

***

The carriage was pulled by two black horses. They were tall creatures with short manes and slender legs, yet strongly built, which showed their many journeys of pulling heavy loads. Eliza went up to one of them letting her hand glide across its thick neck, marvelling at its soft fur and gentle nature. The man sitting in front, their driver, gave her an odd look before grunting something about children and their silly ways. The bustle of feet and calm chatter drew the girl's attention away from the animal.

Victoria and Anne stood talking between themselves, giving neither children their attention. Lucas stood a little to their left, eyeing the large carriage. Then the adults motioned for them, it was time to go. An icy wind blew through them as they entered, picking up the hems of skirts and coats before the door was closed and they started moving. To say the ride was bumpy and uncomfortable, was as much of an understatement as if saying the ground would do anything else than freeze during winter. Eliza feared she would get car sick, or rather carriage sick, by the movements, but a gentle hand on her back tore her thoughts away from it. Anne was giving her a small smile, telling her how much she disliked the ride as well, and that Eliza was to tell them if she needed to step out. Victoria gave a humph at the words, muttering about them already being close to late as it were but gave no other words of discouragement.

The ride was surprisingly short, Eliza had closed her eyes and tried to fight the nausea building in her stomach, and before she knew it, they were stopping. The carriage door opened to her left and the sights and sounds of the city poured in. There were people walking all around them as they exited, none paying the strange group any attention. Lucas stepped closer almost immediately, reaching down and taking hold of Eliza's hand. She squeezed it reassuringly.

"Right, I'll be making my way then, you lot follow Victoria then we'll meet back at a café in about two hours?" Anne turned to look at the children before settling her eyes on Victoria, asking.

Victoria hummed in reply, shooing slightly with her hand at her friend, urging her on and away.

"Yes, yes, that will be plenty of time, shall we say at La Myrtille? You always rave about their pastries…" Victoria answered, just as she turned her back and motioned for the children to follow her. Anne agreed before walking away in the opposite direction.

Eliza held on to Lucas's hand as they walked, trying to keep up with the older woman's brisk pace as she navigated the streets, shops and the people and horses milling about. The young girl kept looking at all the strange things, wanting to see and remember as much of the time she had ended up in, that they almost lost track of Victoria. The older woman gave them an icy glare when she had to stop and wait for them outside an impossibly large and stately building. The mass of brick, stone and ivy looked almost out of place amongst the smaller shops and houses surrounding them. Although it wasn't the only one, Eliza could see other opposing buildings a while away, it was the only one of its kind here, and it stuck out like a sore thumb. As Victoria cleared her throat to get the children's attention, Eliza pulled at the hem of her coat, not knowing what else to do with her free hand.

"Now, as you both have been informed, I expect you both to be on your best behaviour in there. I have an important meeting." Eliza had to fight not to roll her eyes at the words they had heard at least fifteen times already. "And it is quite important that all goes well, understood?" Victoria waited for them both to nod their agreements before continuing. "Good. Now, keep quiet unless spoken to, and if that occurs, keep to *yes* and *no* answers. Excellent!" She clapped her hands together, turned briskly and started up the stairs. Lucas' eyes met Eliza's worriedly. She shrugged in what she hoped was a comforting way before walking up the stairs after the older woman.

The tall building was just as old, lofty and overly fancy as the house they had left. Where they differed was mostly in furniture and colours. The building was covered in heavy, dark wood; from walls to ceiling to the spare furniture and desk lining the walls. The hall they had walked into was vast and higher than that of a church, with a grand chandelier lighting up every crook and cranny. There was a grand staircase winding upwards and on either side of them was a closed door. Huge flower pots filled the empty spaces close to the wall. People in all shapes and sizes, yet dressed immaculately, milled about them at a leisurely pace, giving slight nods and greetings as they passed the little group. Victoria walked right up to one of the desks and started talking to the overly groomed young man standing behind it. When she had finished, Victoria turned around and waved a hand briskly at the two children for them to follow her as she went up the stairs.

Eliza barely had time to take it all in before they were walking down a narrow corridor towards the biggest and most impressive set of doors Eliza had ever seen. The corridor was badly lit, and there were no windows to give natural light. A dark carpet covered the floor. Not seeing the bump in the carpet, Eliza tripped, almost falling flat on her face if not for the hand that had found its way around her waist, holding her firmly. Heart hammering in her chest, Eliza blinked, trying to calm it and find her footing as she looked up at the person who had caught her. Once her footing was found though, the arm disappeared, and Victoria's, *"Huff!"* and *"Be careful!"* was the only evidence she had of it not being an illusion.

Victoria had, by some means, turned around and caught the girl before she could hurt herself. Eliza furrowed her brows in thought as she looked at the retreating woman. *Strange…*

It was a double door; made from a dark, rich, heavy wood with intricate patterns of laurels, ivy and songbirds. Just as they stepped close the doors swung open from the inside by invisible hands, and light flooded their path. A man stepped forward and opened his arms. At first Eliza couldn't see him clearly, but when her eyes adjusted she could see him, and a strange feeling of ice dripping down her spine made her shiver.

"Ah, Victoria, at last we could meet again, I hope your journey was uneventful?" His voice was raspy but not unpleasant.

He had light brown; long, for that time hair drawn back into a small ponytail at the nape of his neck. With a long and slender figure, he stood tall above them, dressed in a frock coat with a waist seam and a full skirt, all in a dark colour. He was dressed in accordance with his wealth and took great pride in his looks; yet was in no way overly handsome. A round jaw and small nose gave him a more childish look than one would expect from his 40 years'. He had such peculiar eyes; almost a yellow-ish amber colour, big yet sharp. He reminded Eliza of an owl, and as if he had heard her thoughts, he sent her a scowl, his lips twitching. Eliza fought hard to keep the blush threatening to creep up her throat from doing so. Lucas' hand found its way into hers again at the exchange.

"Sir Malfort, a pleasure, as always." Victoria answered, as she extended her right hand out towards the man. He took it gently in his and leaned down so his lips almost brushed the back of her hand, yet never making full contact. His strange eyes never left Victoria's as he righted himself and gave a smile that didn't reach his eyes.

It reminded Eliza of a salesperson, the ones who always spoke too long with her parents when they went shopping. All smiles and high voices, pushing with eyes aglow at the prospects of making a sale. Eliza had always thought they acted like vultures or hyenas (she had spent a whole summer watching National Geographic and learnt quite a lot about such animals). This man was no different, she mused.

The grownups had started to walk into the room and it surprised Eliza less and less to see the grandeur of the time. The office, as she guessed it to be, was smaller than the other rooms she had been in the last days, but somehow held more furniture, obstacles and knickknacks then most of them combined. There were three leather couches around the room, a sturdy desk filled with papers, quills and books. A whole section of walls were covered in bookshelves. On the opposite side stood a compact looking closet or wardrobe (Eliza wasn't sure), and all around hung portraits and paintings. None of the faces on the portraits looked nice, but Eliza was starting to see a pattern with that. She was pulled from her thoughts by bumping hard into a small table she hadn't noticed with the sound of something semi-expensive falling, and subsequently, shattering. It hurt and would probably leave a bruise. Victoria and the man, Sir Malfort, had turned to them at the noise and now two sets of eyes bored into hers with different expressions behind them. Victoria's was a mix of shock and anger, while the Owl man, as Eliza wanted to call him, looked the calmer of the two. Only a slight furrow between his brows revealed his feelings, but the downturn of his lips did not bode well. Eliza braced herself for the shrieks and lectures she no doubt would be getting, but when no words or sounds came, she dared to look at the older couple in front of her.

"Are you hurt, child?" asked the Owl man. Eliza hadn't expected his voice to be so calm and the lack of anger scared her more. At least when grown-ups screamed, you knew the whole thing would be over when they calmed down. An already calm, probably angry and unknown man? It was a recipe for nerves and discomfort. It took a while before she remembered to answer.

"N-no, err, Sir..." Eliza fixed her gaze on the floor, not wanting the eyes on her, afraid of what she might say or he might see if she met his eyes.

A *Hmm* was all she got before the man turned, Victoria's arm hooked with his, as he spoke over one shoulder. "No need to fret, child, a servant will clean *that*." His eyes glanced over at the broken vase on the floor.

Eliza could feel her face burning. They were heading for a door that up until that moment had been hidden from view as it looked like just a piece of the wall. Eliza didn't see the door handle until they were right in front of it. The girl wondered at it, and immediately wanted a secret door of her own. She wondered what delicious secrets could be hidden behind a door like that. Mr Malfort turned towards the children and fixed them with a disinterested gaze.

"Now, Mrs Hardbrook' and I have some business to discuss in this room, private matters. You two will sit out here and wait." The man lifted a sprinkled hand towards one of the leather couches before continuing. "We shan't be long, so sit down and try *not* to break anything else in the meantime..." He pointed his round face slightly upwards in a gesture.

Eliza was starting to recognise as dismissive and uninterested. She disliked it more and more. She was trying not to stick out her tongue in silent rebellion at his attitude, but she knew, and feared, Victoria's ire at any sign of uncooperating, so she let it be.

The adults disappeared behind the oh-so illustrious door, and the children were alone. It was as if an invisible load had vanished from their shoulders, and both relaxed immediately. They shared a look before they walked over to the nearest couch and fell into it. Neither knew what to say in the moment, and the silence grew heavy around them, seeping into the room like a fog, tangible and irksome. Eliza fidgeted with her hands, one leg bouncing up and down in a fast rhythm. Lucas moved his eyes over the room, finding nothing to settle on slouching more and more into the seat. It felt as if they were being watched by all the portraits in the room, waiting to tell them if they misbehaved. Eliza met the eyes of one of them, a sourly looking older woman, and she poked her tongue out, content to take out her anger on the inanimate person. Lucas caught the movement and had to suppress a giggle with his hand. The boy found another face on the wall, and contorted his face, puffing out his cheeks, crossing his eyes and lifting his nose. Eliza let out a high snort and bit her lip before turning to meet his eyes, raising an eyebrow challenge — and soon they were facing off, trying to outdo the other in making the strangest and ugliest faces both to the pictures and to each other. Gargoyles, pigs, trolls and misshapen monsters took their places on the couch, and soon their laughter filled the dimly lit room.

The laughter faded as they settled back unto the couch. Lucas removed his coat, claiming it to be too warm and settled it next to him. His finger stroking the fabric as his head lulled to the side, finding Eliza's shoulder, and settling there. He gave a hum of content as Eliza lowered her head onto his. They sat for a minute, finding a little peace, and suddenly the day's ordeal settled back into the girl's mind. Immediately her body tensed noticeably, her shoulders stiffening under Lucas's head. He shifted, leaning more into her as his free hand sought hers. He was about to ask if she was all right when Eliza started talking.

"Do you wonder what we would be doing right now if I hadn't come through that portal?" Her question hung in the air for a moment. Lucas sighed before answering.

"I would probably have been walking the streets, trying to find breakfast, or lunch, or dinner for that matter. Maybe gotten a few of the other boys with me to try and get some bread from the baker down the street. He often leaves the old rolls out to sell at this time, and if we are many enough, and cause a scene, we would probably get our hands on a roll or two…" Eliza's thumb had started to trace a pattern over Lucas's hand nestled in her lap as he spoke. She gave it a squeeze. "And you?"

Eliza knew what she would be doing. She would have had breakfast with her father (her mother always left for work before she awoke), and then he would have driven her to school. Eliza would have been in her math class at this hour, trying to focus and not draw doodles and horses in her book. She had gotten in trouble for that enough times. Yet here she was, in another place, another time, with people who in a very short amount of time had come to mean the world to her. Eliza didn't know if she wanted to laugh or to cry, feeling only a hollowness inside her chest.

A tugging sensation on the lapel of her coat made her look down. A blush creeped up her neck, she had forgotten to answer and had gotten lost in her head again. Lucas's clear, icy blue eyes looked back at her with an understanding and an openness that made her want to cry even more. She had no real reason to feel bad for herself, not when she knew Lucas had it so much harder, yet a sadness had taken place inside her bones. It made her shoulders slump and her eyes grew misty with unshed tears. Were they for him or for her own thoughts that didn't make sense. Had she a right to cry? She didn't know, and she didn't care. Eliza wanted to turn, to fold herself into the boy next to her, have him hold her as she cried and try to understand what her life had become, and if it would ever be normal again; if she would ever get back home again.

The opening of a door made them jump apart. Lucas shifted uncomfortably as Eliza fidgeted with a lock of her hair, uncertain of where she should look. Victoria and the man, Mr Malfort, shook hands before turning towards the children, collecting them as they made their way out towards the main hall. There the man excused himself before walking up to a spindly fellow with twitching hands. They spoke briefly, heads lowered, and the Owl man looked more and more upset about whatever the other man told him. Eliza looked away as Victoria called them, already at the exit and impatiently tapping her fingers over crossed arms. When Eliza looked over her shoulder back at them, the two men were gone. Just as they reached the first steps outside, a sort of whimper sounded from Lucas. Two eyes fell upon him, and he shrunk back on himself.

"I'm s-sorry, missus, but I seem to have forgotten my coat at the gentleman's office." Lucas refused to meet Victoria's eyes as he spoke, focusing rather on a spot by his feet. Eliza could hear the resignation in Victoria's voice even before she spoke, and took a step forward, slightly in between the boy and the older woman, before speaking.

"I'll go with him back in. I'm sure they will let us grab it and go. We'll apologise a lot and don't speak to anyone we meet!" She reached behind her and took hold of Lucas's hand.

Victoria raised a hand, immediately making the boy flinch, but ran it through her pinned up hair, ruffling it, and sighed.

"Very well. I will wait here, you two be quick about it!" She gave them a stern gaze which Eliza was sure could freeze lava, before collecting herself.

With a nod from the older woman, the two were off, jogging through the hallway, up the stairs and into the office. The grand room was empty and seemed more eerie then earlier. Why, Eliza didn't know, nor did she care. She thought they were lucky not to have met anyone on their way. Lucas ran up to the couch and grabbed his jacket with a triumphant smile. Eliza smiled back and nodded her head in the direction of the door.

"Let's go, can't keep the 'missus' waiting!" She snickered.

Lucas rolled his eyes at her, slightly punching her on the shoulder as they made their way to the door.

The sound of footsteps made them stop dead in their tracks. Eliza wasn't sure why she did it, nor what made her think it was a good idea, but as soon as she understood that there were people walking towards them, she grabbed Lucas by the arm. Quickly she glanced around, finding nothing of interest, there, the old cabinet. She pulled the boy along, hushing him when he tried to speak before pulling open the cabinet door. Blood rushed in her ears and her heart was thumping wildly. The cabinet wasn't as big as she had hoped, but it had an under section just big enough if they squeezed together. Eliza crammed Lucas in first before she followed, unfortunately ending up sitting on top of his leg. It was extremely uncomfortable, but as the footsteps closed in, there was no time for adjustments and she closed the door, leaving them in total darkness save the sliver she could see through in the door. The door they had entered in opened and the Owl man and his spindly companion walked through. The Owl man walked at a much quicker pace, leaving the other man slightly jogging to keep up. They were talking from the moment they entered.

"...and it will all collapse! I have told you how important that final contract means to this entire enterprise. Without it, the other deeds are as well as worthless, and *that* makes it all for naught! I will not have my entire reputation and legacy ruined by some sentimental old hag and her need for proper closure."

Mr Malfort was pacing back and forth as he spoke, his hands running through his now unkempt hair, eyes fixated on the poor man who was cowering before him. He looked like a bird of prey, closing in on a terrified fieldmouse.

"We are running out of time, Mackenzie, and time, on this occasion, is most certainly money. The bankers have all lent me vast amounts of their money to see this project to fruition, and we are already behind schedule. If I don't have Mrs Hardbrook's deed to her house by the end of the week, they will want their money back, and with it, my life!" He seemed to be talking more to himself. Twitching his head around the room. The other man, the fieldmouse, took a step towards him.

"But Sir, c-can't we just finish this the way we started? Surely one woman can be dealt with. Her husband's dead; no one would think twice if she fell into despair? Wanting to be with him again? Surely, we can make…"

He was cut off by Mr Malfort's booming laugh. The sound bouncing off the walls like a cannon.

"Isn't one life enough, Mr Mackenzie? Have you grown a bloodlust during our time together? No, she is not just one woman. She is known as a cold-hearted society lady, not one for cheap theatricals such as the taking of one's life. Besides, she has that friend, the lady she lives with, Anne Richards I believe. Mrs Hardbrook has probably left the house to her when she reaches her demise…"

The Owl man had stopped his pacing. He stood in front of the other man, blocking him from Eliza's view from the cabinet.

"No, we can't dispose of her, there would be too many questions. I will have to persuade her. I will set up another meeting, and if she refuses again, I will give her a final offer at my ball this Saturday. I won't lose!" The fieldmouse cowered before the other man, nodding quickly at the temper in his voice.

"We have too much invested in this project, and I shall be damned before I let it slip through my fingers like…"

Mr Malfort had started, but a sound made him freeze. The two men in the room locked eyes, both searching, questioning each other without speaking, all the while knowing neither man had made the noise.

Inside the cabinet, four hands covered Eliza's mouth, eyes stared out in fright and two hearts beat like war drums going into battle. It was her sneeze that had made the sound. All the dust inside the cramped cabinet had been too much, and as she had gasped at the proclamation coming from the tall man outside, the dust settled in her mouth and nose. Lucas's hands had scrambled to cover her mouth, trying in vain to keep the noise in. Her own hands were mere seconds behind his, their task the same. But it was too late. The sound made the two men outside stop speaking and start listening for more noises.

Eliza could feel Lucas's hands tremble against her lips, her own breathing coming out ragged. The fear that had crept up her back was like nothing she had ever felt before, and she hoped that if she made it back, she would never feel it again. Right there, though, she doubted she would ever get back home if they were caught. Eliza, too afraid to move, lest they be heard, tried to look at Lucas through the corner of her eye. He sat slumped against her, not moving save for his short, panicked breath that made his upper body rock slightly back and forth. His eyes went from the small crack in the door, to Eliza and back again. Eliza wanted to take his hands in hers and promise him that they would be okay.

As she thought, she noticed one more thing that terrified her, it had gone quiet. There was no talking, no movement of feet against hardwood floors or heavy carpets, no shuffling or creaking of furniture. Had they left? Were they safe? Could they get out of there and warn Victoria of all that they had heard? Would she believe them? After all that had happened how could she not? After all that had happened, how could she? Eliza was lost in thought.

Suddenly, there was light all around them, too much light. Eliza wanted to scream as she was blinded but found she had lost her voice. Lucas gave a startled cry as a hand appeared from the light and grabbed a hold of his shirt at the neck, effectively pulling him out from their hiding space. Another hand went for her arm, but Eliza managed to throw herself forward, between two legs standing above her and falling unto the floor behind the man she now recognised as the fieldmouse man. The man lunged for her as soon as she found her balance on the ground, grunting with effort as he snatched at her limbs. Eliza scrambled backwards, away from the charging man. To her side she could hear Lucas putting up a fight; yelling of profanities, *thumps* and *umphs* as uncoordinated fists tried to make contact with the man holding him, sometimes hitting, sometimes missing their target. She never took her eyes off the fieldmouse as he closed in on her. He looked uncertain and afraid as he jumped at her, trying to get her pinned to the ground.

A shriek pierced the air just moments before the man moved, and Eliza could see Lucas falling to the ground with a red mark across his cheek and lip. Mr Malfort was clutching the arm that had held on to Lucas — it had a big bite mark at the wrist where blood flowed. The sight gave her a bit of courage she needed, and as the man above her closed in, Eliza kicked out with her leg, hitting the man square in the jaw, making him veer off-course and land beside her. His hands clutched at his sore face as he howled in pain.

Lucas gave Eliza a bloodied grin as their eyes met over the carnage before the boy started to run towards the door. Eliza stumbled up, ignoring her aching backside and leg as she moved. The boy had always been quicker than her when it came to running, and her injured body didn't help her. He was already out the door before she had gotten far enough away from the man on the floor, and she knew it had been a bad idea to let the boy lead the way when she felt a hand close around her ankle, making her sprawl onto the floor, landing with a heavy *thud* that took her breath away.

Chapter 13
Unconventional Allies

Darkness was the first thing Eliza could remember. A different darkness than unconsciousness brought, and a smell of wet, damp wood and salt. Every fibre of her body ached as she started to move, but the small space she found herself in refused to let her stand up or shift her body. Her breathing became shallow and fast as her mind scrambled to figure out what had happened. She remembered Lucas her brave yet skittish friend, oh how she hoped he was all right — and herself hiding in the cabinet, hearing Mr Malfort say such frightening things; it didn't make sense.

Why did he want Victoria and Gerald's house? Would he really try anything to get the woman to sell? Had he... Eliza drew a shaky breath that hurt like tiny blades being dragged up her throat... Had he really killed Gerald? Tears flowed gently and unknowingly down her cheeks, over her trembling lips before collecting on her shirt. The young girl tried to slow her breathing, tried to get her mind into thinking about anything else, but it proved to be more difficult than she imagined. So much had happened in so few days, yet she had never had time to properly feel it all. There was always something or someone popping in or disrupting and distracting her. Now she had time, now she was alone, now she could let down her guard, now she could cry fully and let it all out.

She came to later, how much later she didn't know; it could have been hours, it could have been days — not knowing if she had fallen asleep or fallen unconscious after her tears had stopped spilling. Her head pounded and her legs were asleep. She couldn't remember the last time she had eaten or had water. Eliza moved as best as she could while trying to think back. The last thing she remembered properly after being found was fighting with the fieldmouse man and Lucas running. She wasn't angry with him for leaving, she was glad he had managed to escape, or at least, she hoped he had. That way he might be able to warn Victoria and stop them from selling the house to that vile creature.

'No, stay on the matter; how did I end up here!' Eliza scolded herself. 'I got captured by that man, the helper. He grabbed my leg, I fell and everything went kinda black. Then I remember moving, yes! Something, a bumpy thing, that I got placed in, moved about. Someone was talking right before we moved if I could just remember…'

Fed up by it all, Eliza released a half sigh half growl and shot out her hands, wanting to smash whatever was surrounding her. Anger, fear, confusion and hurt fought inside the girl, biting at her insides and starting fires in her chest. Her fists found wood and she gasped at the pain shooting up her arms. As much as it hurt, she could feel her head become less foggy and more alert at the action, and she struck out again. She could feel the wood shake just as she could feel the warm tinkling of what she assumed to be blood on her knuckles. With her lip trembling and eyes that had run dry of tears, Eliza leaned back with a huff, feeling all her emotions drain out from her broken fingers. It was no use. She was stuck, goodness knows where, Lucas could be hurt, Victoria and Anne could have forgotten about them and gone back to their lives and she would be lost in this place, so far away from home, for all eternity, and no one would know what became of her. A cold seeped into her bones, latching on to her very core. If it was the night starting to roll in or the utter sadness and hopelessness that brought it, she didn't know. All Eliza could tell was that it was her only companion in the darkness, as it lulled her into an unrestful sleep.

***

Voices; grumbling, scratching and unintelligible startled Eliza. Her eyes shot open, frantically searching the space around her. She was in what looked to be an old wooden box, as tall as it was wide with tiny slivers of space between the planks holding it together. It was through one such crack that light filtered through, hitting Eliza's one eye, blinding her slightly before letting her see. At first, Eliza wasn't sure what she saw, having been so long in darkness, but as soon as she got used to it, the exterior of her box became more distinct. From what she could make out, she was trapped in a small storage space. Other crates, boxes and baskets stood up against walls, littered the space in front of her and hid her box almost completely. Then her eye fell upon the men the voices that had awoken her belonged to. They were, simply put, scruffy looking. Tattered clothes that hung on their-albeit strong and broad-bodies seemed to be in need of a good wash. Atop their shirts they had odd looking jackets and leather vests and long pants held together by either string or thick rolls of leather. Eliza had never seen men looking like them before and would have made fun of their strange clothes had she seen them under any other circumstance.

At that moment, the girl was afraid to breathe too loudly and kept one hand lightly pressed over her mouth. What they were talking about, Eliza couldn't make out. They stood too far away. Suddenly, out of nowhere, it felt as if the ground beneath them shifted, rolled and swayed. Eliza's stomach somersaults at the motion, yet neither man seemed to notice the shift in movement. One lifted his strange hat to scratch at his head before nodding to his companion. As suddenly as they had appeared, they moved, opened a door outside Eliza's vision range and were gone. Eliza felt her heart speed up again, for in the few seconds the door had been opened, she had heard something that made her blood rush from her face and hands go clammy. There had been voices, lots and lots of voices, but there had also been the unmistakable sound of crashing waves and seagull cries. The ground's movements made sense then. She was aboard a boat. Fresh tears spilled what was supposed to be a cry and what sounded more like a dry croak erupted from the girl.

Just as the realisation was about to break the last strand of hope and resilience in her, a loud bang shook the entire ship, crate and girl. More voices echoed as feet could be heard rushing about, above beside and below her. Eliza scrambled around, trying to see out of the cracks around her, trying to figure out what was happening, but to no avail. Then, another bang sounded, closer than the last, louder and more threatening. Eliza couldn't help but cry out in fear as she heard the unmistakable sound of wood splintering beside her. Light, too much light flooded her senses. The sounds of people yelling and running all around her made her press herself even closer into the crevice of the wooden box. Her mind was blank, there was too much happening to think, too many noises and too much fear to concentrate. The sound of metal hitting metal, battle cries of victory and pain, and bodies hitting wood mixed in with the sound of Eliza's heavy breathing until it became one. Time seemed to slow even as the noises and lights flashing became quicker and quicker. Her blindness from the box made it all seem so much more intense, never really knowing what was going on, nor where it was happening, nor if she was going to be discovered.

At that moment Eliza didn't know whether she wanted to be seen or not. Would she be saved? Would she be killed? Tears, snot and sweat mixed on the girl's chest as she buried her head down between her knees and under her arms, trying to hide as much of herself as she could. Trying to find comfort in the darkness of herself. She didn't know how long she had been singing to herself, yet as the words of her father's lullaby reached her ears, her breathing started to slow. Pictures of her father and the memory of her singing to Lucas mixed in her head as the song continued, growing stronger with each sentence as the battle raged on outside and the sweet notes clashed with the clanging of metal. For Eliza was sure then, that only a battle could bring such noise and fear.

How long she had stayed in that position, how long she had sung, how long the battle had lasted, Eliza didn't know. Five minutes or five hours? She had tried to forget it all. So, when a sort of silence penetrated the mantra of words and found her ears, her breathing stopped. The only sound then being her heartbeat.

Crack!

The top lid of her box tore open with a deafening noise. Eliza let out a startled scream that broke off too soon from her exhausted body. A huge mass blocked out the light that had filtered in and blinded the girl, towering above her. A voice called out and more shadows appeared. Eliza thought she saw some type of long metal glint in the light before darkness crept over her eyes, stealing her sight and breath away, leaving only the last glint of what looked like an arm moving towards her.

***

Plush pillows, soft fur and a warm blanket. It had been such a long time since Eliza had felt such luxuries around her. She pressed her face more firmly into the pillow, dragged her fingers through the fur beneath her and sighed as the warmth enveloped her.

This must be what heaven feels like — she thought to herself.

Eyes snapped open as her heart skipped a beat. This was all wrong. Why was she surrounded by plushy warmth when the last thing she was near was a hard wooden box? She gazed frantically about her, taking in the room around her. Dark wooden beams, low ceiling and a small window. A desk littered with paper, books, a compass and an old looking wine glass. Eliza was lying in a bed, smaller than the one back at Victoria and Anne's house, but bigger than a child's bed. Pillows lay all around her body, what looked to be a sheepskin was used as a mattress and a purple quilt worked as a comforter atop her. Beside her was a small table where a candle stood aglow, brightening the dark room. The only other light came through the small window.

Standing up Eliza saw that she had been undressed down to her shift and long socks. Her legs wobbled as she placed them on the cold floor, her time in the small box making standing up difficult and unusual.

With small yet strong steps, Eliza moved towards the small round window, determined to see out, and try to figure out where she was. There was a slight rocking motion beneath her feet, but that could mean anything, she hoped. Yet her fears were met as she looked out and saw nothing but dark blue waves and clouds around her. She was still at sea, still on a boat. Was it the same one she had ended up in? Was it another one? Eliza chewed at her bottom lip as she thought, hands running through her loose and wild hair. One of her fingers got caught in a tangle, and she pulled hard to try to get it out. It stung as the hair and finger stayed tangled, and a cry tore from her. Frustration grew inside her, egging her, toying with her and calling her *weak* and *stupid* for getting herself into this mess, and possibly endangering her new friends. She had to escape, had to get away and go home. She had to leave *now*.

Standing close to the only door in the room, ear pressed hard against it, lip between her teeth and breathing shallow, Eliza readied herself for her escape. There were people on the outside, lots of them, but she wasn't afraid, or so she forced herself to believe. She had a plan ready. Open the door quietly, try to find a lifeboat or something else to get away in, sneak out of the room, make a run for it, and if she had to, find something sharp, just in case. Eliza took a deep breath, on the count of three. I will open the door.

One...

Her palms were sweaty.

Two...

Her pulse quickened.

Three!

The door shot open from the force. Eliza barely had time to clamp her hands over her mouth to stop the scream she was about to let out. Her eyes were blinded by the sun, which had at that moment decided to come out from between the clouds. Everything around her had gone quiet, and for a moment, Eliza hoped that she had been wrong, and that she was alone on the deck. She was, however, not wrong. As her sight came back, her surroundings came into focus, and with it, so did the people, frozen to their spots, around her. They looked, for the moment Eliza had to look them over, like just the sort of people one didn't want to be captured by. Although they were all different shapes and sizes, they all had the same look of menace and brutality on their faces. Without thinking, and without a second to spare, Eliza let out what she hoped sounded frightening her loudest war cry. The look of horror on the closest man was enough to spur the girl on. She shot forward on her no longer shaky legs, determined to get away. The people around her sprang into action; leaping, yelling and grabbing at her. She jumped, dodged, feinted and danced her way forward.

One man managed to close his fingers around her dress yanking her backwards and out of her momentum. Eliza turned, threw out her arm, hitting the man straight in the face, making him let go of her. As he stumbled back, she saw something that surprised and delighted her. The man had a sword tied to his waist. Adrenaline fuelling her body and mind, Eliza grabbed the hilt and pulled the sword out. She had not expected it to be so heavy, and her arms crumpled slightly under the weight, yet it did not stop her resolve. Steps closed in on her left side, and she swung around, sword first as she slashed at whoever dared to approach her.

The sound of metal slicing through cloth before hitting wood was new to her, but she found it the least of her problems as more people had started to close in on her. Voices grew as some shouted, both at her and to her, but she paid them no heed. She turned again, slashing, wielding and stepping, hoping to intimidate those who surrounded her. There were so many, crowding her now, and she turned and turned, trying in vain to keep them away. Then metal suddenly met metal with a heavy *clink!* Her momentum and balance lost almost immediately at the contact and she fell to her knees.

Hair blocked her view as she tried to look up. Eliza flicked her hair back over her shoulders, only to feel metal under her chin as her head turned up. Her breathing came out so shaky and heavy that her whole body rocked back and forth, making the blade dig slightly into her skin, but not enough to draw blood. Her eyes struggled to see properly from the angle she was in, looking up at her captor. A voice then broke the silence.

"Thsk, thsk, little one. Who are you to stir the quiet, to upset and threaten my crew unprovoked? and after we saved you! That's bad manners, that is!"

Although rough and strangely tinted, the voice clearly and unmistakably belonged to a woman. Eliza's brows furrowed. Saved her? She had no idea where she was nor who they were. Wasn't *she* the one threatened?

"Showing such disrespect usually ends with a pistol shot, or more efficiently, the plank! Seeing as you're nothing but a young'un, I'll let you off, with a lesson!" The woman stepped back, letting the blade fall from under Eliza's chin.

Eliza wasn't quite sure what she expected the woman to look like, but she wasn't aware how wrong she could have been. Standing above her was a tall woman with long and loose sandy blonde hair, what could have been a reddish brown, old military jacket, loose trousers, a black triangle hat, a huge brown leather belt strapped over the front of her chest down to her hips where Eliza saw the woman would sheath her sword. The hand that held the sword was bandaged with an old, dirty cloth. The woman carried a smirk on her face, and cold brown eyes met the girl before she raised an eyebrow down at her. The sword Eliza had dropped fell back down at her feet with a *clang!*

"Since you want to fight my crew, you'll have to fight me too. Now, pick up the sword, fight me, and I might pardon you!"

As she spoke, the woman turned around and took several steps away from the frozen girl. The people who had surrounded her, had fallen back, lining the sides of the ship. They all carried amused smiles or smug expressions as they watched her.

Eliza didn't know what to do. The adrenaline that had coursed through her had disappeared, leaving her with mind numbing fear. Tears pricked in her eyes and a lump started to form in her throat. She gritted her teeth at the feeling. She was no coward! She had made it this far, endured worse and seen more terror than this! Picking up the sword, Eliza could hear a murmur running through the crowd around them. She took a step forward, meeting the eyes of the woman and gave a short nod. She would not back down. The woman gave a nod back and Eliza moved. She raced forward, raising her blade with both arms, aiming for the woman's stomach. *Clang!* Metal on metal, again. Eliza stumbled back by the force, hair spilling around her face. Up again went the sword, ready to make a mark. *Cling!* The woman parried without even moving her feet, looking as if the whole fight bored her greatly. Eliza growled at the sight, feeling her arms start to tire, but refusing to quit. Again, her arm and sword moved, aiming for the woman's leg, but Eliza stopped herself right before she could be blocked, spun around and swung her sword as hard as she could into the other leg. She hadn't seen the sword turn to the flat side, so when she felt the blade make contact with soft flesh instead of hard metal, the shock made her drop the blade instantly.

The woman let out a surprised yelp as the hit knocked her off balance and a second later, she had one knee on the ground, the other beneath her, sword falling beside her. The look of utter wonder was repeated on the faces of the crew around them. Eliza couldn't help but step forward, raising her empty hand towards the woman.

"Oh, sorry…!" Eliza shut her mouth with a *snap* when her own words registered. Had she just apologised to the woman who was trying to hurt her?

Eliza was shocked when the other woman started laughing. A deep chuckle turned into full-on laughing as she clutched one hand to her stomach. The other waved off the crew who had gathered around her. Eliza didn't know if she should move forward or run back. Then the woman stood up, ran a hand through her hair and looked at the girl with one eyebrow raised.

"One thing to learn, little one, never apologise to the attacker while they still breathe! If they are dead, then, abide by your good manners…" The woman said, her voice lighter from the laughter.

Eliza just stared at the woman, resisting the urge to apologise once again. She instead fiddled with her fingers as she waited for the woman to continue. Eyes locked together, they both wondered what to do next. A man, short and scraggly looking, took a step forward from beside the woman.

"Captain, what are yer orders?" His voice was as scratched as the man looked.

So, the woman was the captain aboard the ship. For it was a ship they were on, no doubt. There were crates, ropes and cases all around them, two huge masts right behind the captain with sails dropped and filled with wind. The ship itself was dark and old, with marks left from work and battle probably all around the rails. Eliza took it all in, as she felt her heart drop into her stomach, the adrenalin fully gone. She was left shivering and scared.

Finally, seeing she was only in her nightgown and socks, she crossed her arms over her frame and hunched her shoulders high up under her ears. The woman, the captain, furrowed her brows in thought before she turned her back and addressed the crew.

"My dear scurvy riddled hounds, it seems we have an unintended guest. She has proven to be highly dangerous, possibly even wild — you can see it in her eyes." The woman's voice rang out, and the crew nodded and grunted in agreement. "Who knows what she might do! Well, you all know what I, nay, what we all feel about such guests?"

The shivering was replaced by ice running down Eliza's body. Fearing the worst, she took a small step back and shrunk slightly in posture. The captain turned and looked straight at the child, face devoid of emotion before a small smile edged its way into the corner of her lips.

"We... Make sure to tell the cook to set another placing at the table."

It was said so casually that at first Eliza didn't hear it. It wasn't until loud *Aye's!* came from the crew that it dawned on her. She looked incredulously at them all, eyebrows raised.

The captain took a step towards her before kneeling. She searched for Eliza's eyes, catching them and held eye contact. Her face grew softer yet her eyebrows furrowed. Shrugging slightly, the captain removed her coat, gently reached out and placed it around Eliza's shaking shoulders. The coat was heavy and smelled strange, but it was warm and stopped the wind from nipping at her bare skin. Eliza felt small where she stood, but something about the woman's eyes made her feel at ease.

"Hmm, what are we to do with you, little one?" As she spoke, the woman glanced over the girl's frame, slightly shaking her head. "You must have a great story to tell..." The captain trailed off before standing up and turning towards her crew.

"All right, back to your work men, I don't pay you to stand around and stare all day!" With that, the crew went off to their work; some climbed the mast, some started to wash the deck, while others disappeared to do who knows what.

The captain turned back and gave a last questioning gaze at the girl before she started to walk. Eliza hurried after, not really knowing what to do or what to say. They walked past the cabin she had woken up in, down a set of stairs to the inside of the ship. On the inside, the ship was warmer. Candles lit up the walls of the huge room they had stepped into. Around them, there were wooden benches, chairs and tables. A few members of the crew sat peeling potatoes while others were polishing swords. A huge man whose dark skin made him near invisible in the dimly lit room, with broad shoulders, tattoos peeking out from under his shirt on both his arms and up his neck and an eye patch, stood as they came closer to him.

"Gibbs, my good man, I'd like to introduce you to our new guest! This is… Oh, it seems neither has introduced themselves properly. I am Captain Chesca Orlow, the captain of this fine ship and crew. If you hear any of these hell hounds say my friends call me Chess, it is a complete lie, and you must tell me immediately so I can have them hung for mutiny!" The man, Gibbs, laughed heartily, one hand clutching his stomach while the other dropped the half-peeled potato on the table.

"Ay, Captain, I reckon you would! We all know there's only one who's allowed to call you that!" His voice was deep and dark with a strange accent Eliza had never heard before. They both shared a secretive look before chuckling. Captain Chesca turned her head to hide her smile. Eliza watched them, her fear having faded, and her curiosity peaked.

"Well, lass, my name is Gibson, you may call me Gibbs, as our fair captain does. I'm the cook aboard this ship." Here, he leaned closer to Eliza, lowering his voice to barely a whisper. "And sometimes, I've been seen playing the flute, if asked nicely…" He gave a conspiring wink, making Eliza giggle behind her hand.

"And who may you be, lass?" Both Gibbs and the Captain Chesca watched Eliza closely as she tried to figure out what of her story to share. She settled on just her name, for the moment.

"I am Eliza Roberts, I don't have a profession yet, but I like to dance and sing and explore!" Her voice was slightly shaky as she spoke. She coughed to clear it up. Gibbs laughed once more; even the Captain Chesca gave a chuckle.

"Now then, little one, I suggest you tell us your story, preferably from the start." Captain Chesca fixed Eliza with a sharp yet friendly gaze. The girl shifted uncomfortably before sighing. Who knew what would happen to her, so why not share her story again?

***

Lucas paced in front of the lit fireplace. His hands moved from twitching at his sides to running through his black and white hair, tugging at strands before falling. He had been pacing since the moment Victoria and Anne had brought him back to the house. The women were in the kitchen, talking amongst themselves. He went over everything that had transpired that day. He cursed himself for running, for letting Eliza out of his sight and not stopping to wait for her. Tears flowed down his reddened cheeks — one with a large, purple handprint. It was in his nature to run to run as fast as he could, and to only stop when he knew he was safe. Out on the street it was every child for themselves in those moments. Suddenly angry, he threw out his leg, aimed at nothing, but hitting the end leg of a table. It hurt when his toes met the wooded leg, but it only fuelled his rage.

Why, why, why? — until he felt two arms wrap around him and knees pressing against his back. Gently, the arms pulled him back, with more strength than he would have given the woman credit for and placed him on her lap. Anne held him tightly to her with one arm, while the other stroked down his side. She hummed low, whispering sweet words and shushes into his ear. Lucas's breath became steadier with each second. He felt inexplicably safe in the woman's arms. He noticed that she smelled like a flower field and was as warm then as any summer day he had ever experienced.

Anne rocked slowly from side to side, unsure of what exactly to do, but wanting nothing more than to comfort the poor boy. He hadn't stopped crying since she had run into him and Victoria outside the café earlier. When he told her, through hiccups, what had transpired, it felt as if all the air around them vanished. Victoria had stood there, not saying much as the boy talked, but with a growing fury in her eyes and her jaw so clamped shut her teeth might have cracked.

Hurriedly, they had made their way home. It had not been easy. Victoria had wanted to rush back into the building, declaring war upon those who would stand in her way, and get the girl back; but the door to the building had been guarded from the moment Lucas had appeared. He had found a backdoor as he escaped, running around the massive building until he nearly crashed into Victoria, and with what little breath he had left, he told her what had happened. They had met up with Anne and got a coach to drive them home.

Now, several hours and kettles of tea later, they were gathered in the Hardbrook living room. Lucas, curled up in Anne's embrace, had fallen silent. Victoria had entered and resumed the boy's pacing. Anne could see the invisible smoke fuming out of the other woman's ears. Her face as stone cold as the 'grounds' to the house. Anne knew there were more emotions at war inside Victoria than the woman let show. Suddenly, Victoria stopped in front of them and threw up her hands.

"What are we to do!? We can't just sit here and dwindle! And you, boy, are you certain you heard correctly?" Victoria's voice was as near hysterical. She pointed at Lucas with a trembling finger.

Anne shot her dear friend an ice-cold glare. How dare she take that tone at the poor boy? Couldn't she see his duress? She ran her fingers through the boy's hair as he started to shake again.

"Victoria, what do you expect us to do? march up to Mr Malfort's house and demand he let Eliza go? For all we know, she could have escaped and is wandering the town, all alone, and is both frightened and cold! Or he could have taken her some place…" Anne's voice was barely above a harsh whisper. She didn't want to frighten the boy in her lap any more, yet he had started to cry again as she spoke, making her shut her mouth place a chaste kiss to his temple.

Victoria pinched the bridge of her nose with two fingers, sighed, and started to walk again. She was furious, but at whom, she was uncertain. She was angry at her friend for allowing the children into their lives in the first place. She was angry at the girl, for showing up and for getting herself into more and more dangerous trouble. She was angry at herself, for not following the children inside to retrieve the coat that now lay in a heap by the entrance at the door. Now, was not the time to be outraged over the past, nor to throw blame. It was time to sit down and figure out what their next step would be.

"Lucas, I need you to sit down, and tell us both what transpired and what *exactly* you heard." Victoria knew they had been told already, but she needed clarity, and knowledge to think clearly.

The boy looked up from his seat on Anne's lap, met the other woman's eyes, and nodded. He was afraid of being yelled at again, but he knew that Eliza's life depended on him in that moment and he pushed through.

Hours later, Victoria and Anne sat close around the small kitchen table. The boy, exhausted from the day, had finally fallen asleep on one of the couches in the living room. Anne had placed a blanket over him before returning to the kitchen. Neither woman spoke, for neither knew what to say. A silence had taken over the room; pressing, nearly deafening. It held the women captive. Inside, they were not so quiet, for both sat with their own inner battles. Words, arguments, ideas, they were all there, yet none of them were clear or concise, and neither dared share. The still full teacups stood forgotten before them, now just as cold and useless, as both women felt.

***

Evening had come, dulling out the sun's warmth and light, leaving the boat and its crew in a lull of ever-growing darkness. The ship and the sea seemed to be so dark that they flowed together. Aboard the ship, however, there was light from the candles lining the walls, and the fire in the kitchen. There was a sound of music and chatter. The entire crew, save for the old man steering the ship, were gathered below deck after their meal. There had been loud conversation, food and drink going from table to table, and a lot of attention paid to the little girl who now sat beside an animated captain.

The girl's big eyes were glued to her dining companion, who were in the middle of a retelling of a particularly great adventure. One of the Captain Chesca's hands held a big glass of wine, the other her unsheathed sword flew, spilling fluids and nearly knocking off another sailor's hat. Eliza would have laughed at the action, had she not been as captivated as she was. When Captain Chesca finished, she stood up piercing her sword nearly through the table — there came cheers, whoops and laugher from the crew around them. Eliza clapped her hands together, asking question after question, her eyes never leaving Captain Chesca.

"Oh Captain Chesca, you really are brave! Did you *really* steal a bag of gold from right under a sleeping king?" Eliza asked.

Captain Chesca laughed as she leaned over and rested her free hand on the girl's shoulder.

"I did indeed, my little one! I just made it back to my ship when his cry of rage sounded throughout his ship and awoke his guards!" Captain Chesca answered with a wink.

"Wow…!" Was all Eliza could say. Her eyes then fell on the sword as Captain Chesca tugged it out from the wooden table.

"Do you think you could teach me how to use that?" Eliza bit her lip as she asked.

Captain Chesca looked to be pondering the question for some time before locking her eyes with the girl.

"Aye, I don't see why not! You proved yourself to be quite adapt already, so it'll be an easy task. I recon you'll be quite the master before we get you home!"

Eliza jumped up from her seat, squealed loudly before throwing herself onto the other woman. She poured out many thanks as she held on to her as tightly as she could. Captain Chesca, slightly startled, just patted the girl on the back. Out of the kitchen then came the cook, an old towel draped over his shoulder, and a small blonde woman Eliza hadn't seen before. She was not much taller than the girl herself, with long, straight blonde hair and dark green eyes. Her lips were a type of pink Eliza hadn't seen any other woman in this time wear. She wore a blue dress, similar if not simpler to the one she had seen Anne wear. Eliza also noted that she was the only one on board wearing a dress. Even Captain Chesca and some of the other women wore trousers. The woman smiled broadly as they came towards the captain's table. The room had become quiet. Gibbs then cleared his throat and asked a simple question.

"Are you lot ready to dance?"

The room erupted in *Aye's!* and cheers.

A low drumbeat started. Some of the crew scattered from near the end of the room to show a man sitting by a large instrument Eliza couldn't name. His hands beat it, creating the beat. As other members started to push and lift tables and chairs out of the way, the blonde woman who had been standing with Gibbs moved over the floor to join the man. She picked up a fiddle and started to play. Eliza had never heard such a playful sound, the woman played with such life, tapping her foot to the beat while moving her whole body with each draw of her bow. She smiled at the man playing the drum. It looked as if they played off each other, one following the other while trying to outdo each other. Others started to stamp their feet and vocalise to the music. Gibbs then joined in, pulling a flute like object from his pocket. Eliza couldn't help but smile at the sight. Soon there were people on the floor, twirling, stomping and jumping in time with the music.

Captain Chesca bent down beside the girl, who had not noticed the woman moving closer and jumped slightly as the captain reached out a hand towards her. Eliza was a little unsure, but the swell of music, the cheers from the crew and the easy smile of Captain Chesca soothed her. With a nod, they clasped hands and moved into the circle of dancers. The steps didn't matter that much, Eliza soon realised, if one moved with the beat and claps of those who didn't dance. The room filled with song, the hypnotic sound of clapping and stamping and the pure happiness that only dance could bring. People danced together in pairs and in singles, moving around each other with practised ease. Eliza could see the small blonde woman dancing around as she played, how, Eliza couldn't fathom. How someone could play so beautifully *and* dance with high kicks and twirls was beyond her.

Soon she was twirled from the captain to another member of the crew as Captain Chesca joined hands with two others. They danced on a line, sideways, with kicks and smiles on their faces. Then they all moved to make a circle in the middle of the room, all holding hands as they moved. *Step step hop! Step step turn direction. Step step hop!*

Eliza let out a peel of laughter as she was twirled around again. Then, all too suddenly, the music stopped. Applause and cheers sounded. For the first time in too long, Eliza's mind wasn't troubled or plagued by her past. The only thing she felt in that moment, was happiness, and her feet a little sore.

***

Morning came with caws of seagulls and the sound of people at work. Eliza once again found herself in the little bed surrounded by pillows and blankets. She hadn't remembered falling asleep, just sitting with the Captain Chesca, and Gibbs while the woman played the violin. In the dimly lit room, Eliza had no idea of how late into the evening they had talked, so it could have been way past her usual bedtime. She had learnt that the woman who played for them was named Lavinia, and that she couldn't speak. When Eliza had asked why, Gibbs had told her that a sea witch had stolen her voice when she was a child. Lavinia had given him a small shove at that before signing something with her hands. Captain Chesca explained that Lavinia had never spoken but used her hands and her music to communicate. Lavinia was a delightful woman, with many stories to share.

Captain Chesca had spoken while the woman moved her hands and contorted her face into different emotions. Eliza was told that the room she had awoken in belonged to Lavinia. She had immediately thanked the woman and apologised for stealing her bed. Lavinia had just laughed and smiled as she waved it off.

The evening was filled with laughter and stories. Eliza had even been shown how to play the violin. It hadn't sounded too good, but she was delighted at having tried.

Stretching and rising from the bed, Eliza found a few articles of clothing lying on the chair by the bed. There was a long-sleeved shirt that at one point had been blue and trousers that were almost as tall as she was. The boots she had gotten from Anne stood by the chair. Her heart sunk in her chest at the sight of them. Anne, Lucas and Victoria. How had she forgotten them? She hadn't, not really, but the last day had been so strange and new that they had been placed far back in her head.

She shook herself. Now was not the time to be angry at oneself. She dressed as quickly as she could, rolling the legs of her trousers up so as not to trip on them. A pair of suspenders lay underneath them and she fastened them so as not to drop her trousers. All ready, she went outside to start the day.

The cold wind hit her right in the face as she opened the door. Even though the sun shone in the sky, it was clearly October, and Eliza longed for her warm coat, scarf and gloves. She needed to find Captain Chesca and ask her how she could return to the mainland. As she walked on deck, several of the crew greeted her. She waved and called *hello* back. Eliza found Captain Chesca at the front end of the ship, looking out on the sea, lost in her own thoughts.

"Good morning captain!" Eliza called out. The woman jumped, slightly startled.

"Ah, good morning, little one. Ready for a new day?" Captain Chesca asked.

Eliza nodded, her loose hair bobbing up and down with the motion. Captain Chesca moved closer before placing her arm around the girl's shoulders. Eliza wanted to ask the woman about her returning, but she didn't want to sound nagging. What if the captain would be hurt by her wanting to leave? Would she be angry? Would she not let Eliza leave? She was brought out of her thoughts by them stopping. Captain Chesca moved to stand before her and unsheathed her sword. Eliza took a frightened step back at the action.

"Yesterday I promised I would teach you a little about sword fighting. I am a woman of my word, and as I have made the ship turn its course, and we should be back at land by nightfall, now, I fear, will be the only time to do so." As Captain Chesca finished, she was startled by having two small, yet strong, arms locked around her waist. Eliza hugged the woman tightly, pressing her face into the woman's side.

"So, this means I'll get to go home?" Eliza asked, muffled though by her face not leaving the woman's side.

Eliza felt two arms wrap around her, hugging tightly. She stepped back and looked at the woman. She saw only warmth and care on Captain Chesca's face. The older woman lifted one hand and cupped the girl's face, moving her thumb across her cheek.

"Yes, little one, you will go home."

No one had told Eliza how gruelling hard just holding a sword up in the right angle was. Not to mention moving her body and sword for a long time. Sweat dripped down her face and her breath came sharp as fog, following them around as they moved. Captain Chesca was a determined and strict teacher, yelling out moves, corrections and comments as they danced around each other. Once again, they were fighting all over the ship. They ran rampant, fighting, ducking, and Eliza was trying — to take cover. The crew jumped out of the way for them, some laughing while other swore at their fighting. One even climbed up the mast to escape one of Eliza's wrongly timed swings with the sword. Hours had passed, and Eliza could feel her body slowly giving up. Yet she was not one to give up and pushed through her fatigue and soreness. Trust, parry, jump to the side. Back and forth they went until one blow to her sword sent it flying out of Eliza's hands. With hair covering most of her face and a shirt soaked through, Eliza found herself at a loss. She was still breathing heavily as Captain Chesca reached out a hand to the girl, pulling her up to her feet. Eliza got a pat on her shoulder and a broad grin from the woman.

"Not bad, little one, I think you're improving!" Captain Chesca's voice was filled with pride.

Eliza gave a lopsided smile at the praise. A shout came from the top of the mast then, and every head on deck turned upwards to see the crew member at the top waving his hand. Eliza knew what it meant, they were close to land. Hope flared in her chest, as dread pooled in the pit of her stomach. She would have to say goodbye to the people on the ship soon. She cast her eyes up to meet those of Captain Chesca's who was still smiling down at the girl.

"Are you ready to go home now?"

Eliza could have sworn Captain Chesca's voice was slightly shaky, but decided not to bring it up. Instead, she gave a nod, and the captain, still with her arm around the girl's shoulder, brought her back into the room below deck. It was time to plan a course for her return.

Chapter 14
Greetings and Grieving

Eliza stood outside the house and fought to regain her breath. The house was dark, only one small candle was lit in the bottom window. It must be the kitchen, she thought. The journey from the ship to the front step of the old house had been an adventure.

She had stood on deck, watching the fog roll by in the ever darkening night, one hand clasped together with the captain's hand, and the other in Gibbs'. They had gone over the plan several times, until they were sure Eliza knew it by heart. At the docks, they would meet with Captain Chesca's Land Man — the person who transported and sold all the crew's wares and supplies who would transport Eliza as far and as close to the house as they could. From then, Eliza would be on her own to get back home. If by any chance they were stopped by police or others, Eliza would hide if she could, then escape. The journey would take several hours at best and the chances of being stopped were high.

After a teary goodbye to the crew, Eliza, Captain Chesca and Gibbs had climbed down into a small rowboat that would transport them to the shore. Had the big ship been spotted by those working on the docks, the police would have been sent for and the plan would have failed. The trek across the nearly black water took longer than Eliza would have guessed, and how Gibbs saw where they were going in the darkness was beyond her. As they reached the shore, Captain Chesca and Eliza jumped from the boat onto land. Eliza waved a final goodbye to Gibbs, then they started moving.

As quickly as they could, they moved along the shore up to the streets. Large buildings lined the dock, and several men were hard at work lifting, shoving and hauling large boxes to be loaded onto ships lined up around them. Eliza could hear her heart beating as she and Captain Chesca stood behind a box, waiting for some of the men to pass them by. With a nod of the captains head, they were off again. Near an empty street, where the lamp light was low, stood an old, slightly rough, carriage. A bored looking horse was at its front and a figure leaned up against it. As silently as they could, they ran up to it. The figure, dressed all in black; a long leathery looking jacket, long trousers, black boots and a large hat, looked up at them as they got closer. The figure nodded to Captain Chesca and the captain nodded back before stopping and turning to Eliza.

The look in Captain Chesca's eyes held so much emotion that Eliza felt frozen to the ground. Eliza could feel fresh tears well up in her eyes at the sight and rushed in for one final embrace. Captain Chesca took a step back after a moment, placed her hand on the girl's cheek, wiping away a tear with her thumb before giving a final smile. Then, as quickly as Eliza felt her hand Captain Chesca took off the way they had come.

Now alone with the strange figure, Eliza felt the fear that the adrenaline had pushed away, come back with a vengeance. She turned towards the figure who was watching her with a bored expression. The figure then tilted his head towards the carriage, signalling for Eliza to get in. She looked back at the person, then at the carriage before moving closer. The carriage was as old on the inside as it was on the outside. A few boxes that looked to have been thrown in haphazardly lay all around. Since there were no seats, Eliza decided to sit in the middle of the floor, with one particularly big box to hide behind.

As soon as she was comfortable, the carriage started to move. The ride was bumpy, long and most unpleasant. Eliza could feel herself being shaken and bumped around with no care for her welfare. At one point they hit a hole in the ground, causing one of the stacked boxes to come tumbling down on top of her. She had to restrain herself from yelling profanities at the driver. At some point in their long ride, Eliza managed to fall asleep. For how long was unclear, but the sound of other carriages and people's voices woke her up with a start.

Were they going to be stopped? she wondered. From her position on the floor, she couldn't see out, but she could feel they were still moving, and the carriage remained dark, so it wasn't morning yet. Then they stopped moving. Eliza's poor heart worked overtime as she heard movement outside and a *thump* she assumed to be the driver jumping from the carriage unto the ground. Without a word, the carriage door flew open, and the strange driver stood in front of her.

"You walk now…" The driver's voice was gruff and course, yet light. Eliza couldn't tell if it was a man or a woman, but at that point she didn't care. On wobbly legs, she got up from her hiding place and jumped out of the carriage.

Eliza ran. She wasn't quite sure if she was running in the right direction, but something inside of her told her that it didn't matter. She just needed to run. Everything ached, there was no breath left in her body and the thumping sound of her racing heart thundered in her head.

Follow the road, look for landmarks she could remember, look out for other people.

The mantra repeatedly sounded along with her heartbeat, fighting to be heard over the *thud, thud, thud.* Had she been running for five minutes? Or five hours? There was no way to tell. Trees rushed past her, blending into one large mass of wood surrounding her.

There were no more emotions, no more tears; she had left them all in her troubled sleep in the carriage. Eliza ran, ran and ran. Until she stopped. Eliza stopped outside a light blue house with eighteen windows and flowers growing all around. Only one room had a light flickering inside of it, all the others were as dark as the night. Her whole body shook with every breath she took.

For some reason, Eliza found out she could not move another inch, not even wriggle her fingers. Most of her wanted to run up the stairs, drag open the door and throw herself into the arms of the first person she saw, but fear had other plans. Eliza could imagine screams, cruel words, hatred and anger from those inside, those she had left behind. Was Lucas in there? Was he waiting for her, safe with Victoria and Anne? Or was he somewhere different, hidden away like she had been? Ice-cold dirt met her knees as Eliza fell. She had no control over her body, no way of saving herself from the bone-cracking impact that met her. She was so cold, so tired, that all fight, all spirit in her disappeared with a long exhale. And in that breath, what Eliza feared would be her last words, she called out for her new family. One by one, their names left her mouth.

Anne… Gerald… Victoria… Lucas…

***

Anne had been pacing by the windows for the last hour. Her hands fidgeted with either her locket usually hidden under her jacket or a loose strand of her curly, brown hair. She had refused to sit down or go to bed, as Victoria had requested nearly three hours earlier. Something in her would not let her rest. It was as if something in her had taken command and demanded that she be present and alert that evening. It had infuriated her companion no end and she chased the woman to her bedroom. Yet Anne knew that the other woman was lying awake. She knew her that much. The boy lay asleep on the couch still, and she didn't have it in her heart to wake him, even if just to move him upstairs. No, he needed his rest, and who was she to deprive him of that? Yet how she longed to have another soul with her that night, even just to breathe in the same room as her, just to feel their presence as her mind tormented her, and her own heart betrayed its master. She cared for the child, as if she had been her own.

Victoria had scoffed at the notion, reminding her, that first night, that the children were not farm animals she could save from the cook and hide in the attic. No, the children would have to go back to wherever they had come from; sooner rather than later and that it would scorn her heart lest she be careful. Yet, she had not, and her heart had welcomed the children in and made such a huge space for them, that now felt oddly empty. It yearned, cried and shook with fear, her old heart, because one of her dearests was missing.

There was, however, nothing she could do at that moment, as Victoria had told her on numerous occasions during the evening, and her heart bled for the children. It refused to listen to the other woman's pleas. So, Anne would walk. She would walk by the window all night, and all day if she had to.

Then there was a *thud,* of what sounded like a plant falling over in the garden, which drew her out of her pacing. Her head shot up to try and see out the window, but the darkness had grown so black, all she could see in the glass was her own blurry reflection. Then something tugged at her heart. As if a string had been woven around it and was now pulled taut. Anne dared not think, lest reason would stop her in her tracks.

She moved as quickly as she dared, out the kitchen, into the grand hall and wrenched open the door. The night air stole her breath away as it knocked against her short yet robust frame making her take a step back into the hall, but the sight before her had her running forward without a moment's hesitation. A shriek ripped through her as she threw herself on the ground next to the small frame. The icy ground ate through her dress and stole the warmth right from her body. Tears gathered in her eyes as her hands fumbled to draw the tiny figure closer to her. With hands shaking, Anne pushed the mess of wild, brown curls out of the girls face to get a closer look, to see what in her heart, she already knew to be true. With a weary smile spreading across her face, she blinked away the tears. Her little girl was back.

Chapter 15
The Last Plan

Lucas shot upright at the shout, his chest heaving and his eyes, wild with panic, scanned the living room. He had heard the front door being pushed open, and Anne's frazzled voice calling out for him. He rushed from the couch he had been sleeping on and went out into the front hall. There he saw Anne holding an unconscious Eliza in her arms. He had no idea that the small woman was strong enough to carry the girl, but at that point, he didn't stop to ask questions. He ran forward, whispering the girls name, and looking first at the girl, then at the woman, silently asking if she was all right. Anne nodded, her breath still coming fast as she stood in the doorway.

"What in all the layers of hell is going on…" Victoria stopped abruptly at the bottom of the stairs. She was woken by a noise, her restless slumber broken, and had made her way downstairs to see what had happened. To say that she had expected to see a slightly deranged looking Anne holding what looked to be a sleeping Eliza in the middle of the night, would have been quite wrong.

Victoria rushed forward, pulling Anne and the girl further into the house, shutting the door behind them. They moved as if one, all three, to the living room, where Anne laid Eliza gently down on the couch that Lucas had been resting on. Even when the girl was out of her arms, Anne's hands never truly left her. She tucked a strand of wild hair behind the girl's ear. She removed the girl's shoes before pulling a blanket over her small frame. She sought out one of the girl's hands and laced her fingers with her own.

Lucas stood by Eliza's feet, eyes moving over her face, her body, trying to see if she was hurt in any way. His hands twitched by his side. He longed for her to open her eyes, to look at him and smile, to hug him close and tell him everything was going to be all right. He had no tears left to cry, he had no more words to say, all he wanted was to hold her and to be sure that she really was here, and that it was not all a dream.

Victoria moved around the couch, too nervous to stand still, and asked Anne a thousand questions. Anne, to her credit, tried to answer as many of them as she could. After being asked what had happened for the third time, the younger woman snapped.

"How should I know what happened? I have told you, I heard a noise, I went outside, I found her collapsed on the ground and I brought her in. I know just as much as you do!" Anne's voice was sharp but held no real anger.

Victoria jumped slightly at the outburst but softened her usually sharp face and placed a hand on her dear friend's arm.

"I know, and I apologise. I… I just want to…" Victoria didn't need to finish her sentence. Anne placed one of her hands atop Victoria's and gave a small smile.

A grunt and some shuffling pulled all of them back to look at the girl on the couch. Eliza's eyebrows furrowed as she exhaled. Then, slowly, she opened her eyes. Anne drew in a breath as Eliza looked at her. The confusion on the girl's face was quickly replaced by surprise, then wonder, before happiness took over.

She shot up from the bed before throwing her arms around Anne. The woman laughed, she laughed with an ease that surprised her. Then Anne felt another set of arms wrapping themselves around them and looked to find Lucas burrowing his head on Eliza's shoulder. The warm comfort that was Victoria's hand settled on her free back. In that moment, no one in the room was frightened, angry or sad. They all felt a warmth growing inside; starting with Eliza, who felt it all over, then Lucas who felt the warmth in his chest and arms, before it moved to Anne, who felt it on her back and on her cheek. Finally, it seemed that the warmth made its way to Victoria, where the heat started in her hand, and moved all the way up, into her heart.

***

They gathered around the kitchen table for hours. The wind had picked up and a lively storm was roaring outside the window. After the clock struck four in the morning, the children, with sleepy and half determined arguments, had been sent to bed. The adults had remained by the table, going over the details of the plan. Anne, with a quill jutting out from her done up hair, chewed at her bottom lip as her eye's roamed over the plan they had written down. Her fingers twitched and stroked at the ends of the paper. Victoria, still in her nightgown, paced behind her friend, thinking of all the terrible things that could go wrong, and all the ways to prevent certain doom. The plan, in theory, was quite simple.

Victoria and Anne had each received an invitation to Mr Malfort's ball. They would go, behaving as if nothing was the matter, and spend as much time around their host without causing suspicion. Meanwhile, Eliza and Lucas would sneak in with the other servants, drivers and grooms. Then they would have to find Mr Malfort's office, locate the evidence they needed and get out without being spotted and hide in the carriage until the ball was over.

As said, the plan was simple, it was the execution and the uncertainty of people that made them all worried. The children had fretted themselves into a walking nervous state, and it would do them no good if they were all too tired or worked up when the time to leave came. The only reason the two women hadn't retired for the night, well, by then morning, was that they had a final matter to discuss, away from the children. Anne turned towards Victoria with a sigh.

"All right, I see no further need to study our plan. Do you have everything ready?" Anne's voice was hoarse, and she felt exhausted.

"Yes, and I will be going into town in a few hours to settle the last thing we agreed upon. Are you sure you do not wish to alter yours?" Victoria's eyes searched her friends face for any signs of, what… She didn't know.

Anne gave her dear friend a tired, small smile. "I already have…"

This confused Victoria, when would she have had the time? Her eyebrows drew together in a frown, as it often did when she was thinking. Anne stood up from the table with a laugh and moved to smooth out the wrinkles in Victoria's forehead. They shared a smile as their eyes met. For the longest time it had just been them. Now they had two children to take care off, at least for a little while longer. But who knew? Maybe Eliza would never find her way home? Maybe Lucas would run away? Maybe they would never see them again after the ball? So much hung in the air, and it was crushing both women, filling them with despair and uncertainty. Yet, they stood there, willing to fight for their home, their late beloved husband and friend Gerald, and the children who had become a part of their lives. The clock hit seven, and Anne sighed. It was time to get everything ready, for soon they had a ball to go to.

***

If someone had told Eliza just a week before, that she would become used to seeing and learning how to properly use nineteenth century clothing, she would have told them they were mad. Yet now she stood, helping Victoria and Anne to get dressed in their brand new dresses for the ball. Exquisite dresses in silk, one dark blue with long sleeves and embroidery and one in baby pink, with short puffy sleeves and a bow. They looked like royalty, and had it not been for the occasion, Eliza would have loved one of her own.

"You both look so beautiful!" Eliza couldn't help but say, her hands trailing over the skirt of Anne's pink gown.

Anne smiled her warm smile at her and patted the girl's cheek affectionately. Eliza herself was back in an old short dress Victoria had asked to borrow. It wasn't half as pretty as what the women wore, but she wasn't going to the ball to dance as a guest, she was on a mission. So, the dress, which stopped a little below the knees and had no long strings or ruffles, was good to run and climb in. She had tried it out outside just be sure, running around the yard with the rabbit. Each of the women had fixed their hair up and away from their face and put on a light hint of makeup. Then they were finished and ready to go.

***

The outside of the mansion was filled with carriages, people dressed in gowns and suits, and torches lining up the gravel path to the front door. Eliza and Lucas studied the entrance as Victoria and Anne made their way in. The children had leapt from the back of their carriage just as it turned into the road leading up to the mansion and ran into the surrounding trees for coverage. They would wait, as planned, to enter the house once everyone had arrived and the servants had gone inside. Then they would make their way inside and find the office and search for the evidence they needed. Once that was secured, Eliza and Lucas would return outside and wait in the carriage until the women left.

Eliza went over the plan in her mind, as she looked over the mansion, trying to find the best way in. The mansion was the largest she had ever seen. It had dark brick with large windows obscured with drapes, and just above the entrance, well-kept ivy crept upwards. To Eliza, the ivy, as it climbed up and draped around the two windows above the door, resembled a skull. She shivered at the sight. Beside her, Lucas gently bumped his shoulder against hers. She looked at him. He gave her a reassuring smile which she returned. She could feel the sweat that drenched her hands and slowly trickled down her back. A slight headache made itself known behind her left eye. How long they sat and waited, Eliza didn't know. It felt like hours as the frozen ground thawed under her knees, drenching her high socks. Lucas shivered slightly, his new old coat, both too big and too thin, barely kept the cold out when he moved. Sitting still for so long had him freezing. The sound of heavy doors shutting startled the two children from their daze and they looked up. The outside of the house was empty. It was time to move.

Slowly, the two of them moved forwards. The mansion seemed to buzz with life, and the light from inside guided them towards the walls. As they moved, Eliza could see that there was no other entrance to the house besides the main door. Lucas whispered something about a servants' entrance, but Eliza couldn't see one. They made their way around the mansion, looking for a door, or an open window. It wasn't until they made their way to the farthest wall that Eliza spotted it. An open window. She let out a frustrated sigh. Of course, it was on the second floor. The children shared a look. Eliza felt the hope seep out of her until Lucas nudged her. By the corner of the wall, ran a rain gutter. Eliza's eyes widened, she loved to climb, but heights weren't her strong suit. She looked it over. It looked secure, sturdy, and she tugged on it to see if it could hold their weight. With time running out, and the lack of options, Eliza saw no other way.

They started to climb. Her hands burned holding on to the freezing metal and she yearned for her soft woollen mittens back in her own time. As they climbed, the music from inside the house could be heard from the open window. *Good,* Eliza thought, that way the noise of their footsteps wouldn't be heard. As she reached the second floor, she made the mistake of looking down at Lucas. The boy was right behind her, but the height made her nauseous, and she pulled herself tight against the wall.

"Eliza!" Lucas whispered harshly. "Eliza, move!"

The girl forced herself to breathe before moving to grab on to the nearest windowsill. The open one was two windows to her left, and she had to cross a very narrow brick ledge to get to it. Eliza swallowed hard, took a deep breath, and moved. Slowly, gently, she edged her way forward. Her fingers grasped whatever they could find as she moved. After the second window, she heard more then saw Lucas joining her on the ledge. They crept forward until finally, she reached the open one. Eliza poked her head through the window to see if the coast was clear before, quite literally, tumbling inside. She had seen no other way in than to go in head first and had fallen onto her back when she landed. Luckily, the music swelled, and she barely even heard herself fall. Lucas joined her shortly after.

They had ended up in a hallway. To their right, they could see a stairway leading down to the first floor. To their left, the hallway stretched far with closed doors lining the wall. The children shared a glance then started moving. They each picked a door and tried to see if it would open. A closet, a bedroom and a library later, there were only two doors left. Eliza picked the door closest to her, and Lucas took the last one in the hall. She tried to open it, but it was locked. Cursing under her breath, she turned to see if Lucas had had any luck. He was nowhere to be seen.

Eliza stepped towards the last door and peeked inside. Lucas stood hunched over a bedside table. It was another bedroom; smaller than the last one, and way more cluttered. The boy was opening drawers and moving objects away, seemingly looking for something. Eliza took a few steps towards him.

"What are you looking for?" She asked.

Without looking up, the boy answered...

"A key, or a notebook, or something that can give us a clue..." He stopped and scratched his head. "I'm not really sure, it's more of a hunch, really."

Eliza explained about the locked door and insisted that the office must be behind it. Why else lock it? Lucas agreed, and together they started talking about how to get the door open. Eliza started searching amongst the scattered objects on the ground. She was just about to inspect some smelly old shirts when Lucas gave a triumphant gasp. Eliza twirled to look at him. He had found a key. As Eliza joined him and took the key herself, Lucas looked around the room one final time. The girl was starting to wonder if the boy had been a detective in a past life, for he had just started to look around when he darted towards the bed. Before she knew it, he had thrown himself down on his stomach and was halfway under the bed before he clambered out. Lucas looked so pleased with himself that Eliza couldn't help but to give the dear boy her biggest smile. She had no idea what he had found, but it didn't matter in the moment.

With a cocky grin, the boy waved a book in his hand, mouthing out the words *secret diary*. Eliza rolled her eyes at him and was about to tell him to put it back when he opened it and started to read. As he read, his smile started to vanish. Lucas flipped the pages, back and forth as he read, before looking up at Eliza with huge, horror filled, eyes. It felt as if ice-cold water ran down her back.

With shaky steps, she moved towards the boy. He said nothing, only pointed at a paragraph in the book. It was a handwritten journal, seemingly filled with personal information. The paragraph Lucas had pointed to was written several months ago. As Eliza read, anger and fear fought inside of her. The handwriting was small but neat, easily enough to read, and entailed, in detail, how and when Mr Malfort had planned Gerald's murder.

It was obvious that Mr Malfort himself hadn't written it, but the detailed information and execution of the plan must have been written by someone close to the man. Someone, like an assistant. Eliza could feel hot tears stream down her face, blurring the written lines on the page. This was it. This was proof of the man's cruel and devious nature. Eliza was sure of it. Until Lucas pointed out, that technically, it was just words written on paper, and that they needed the business transactions from the sale of the women's house to put him into the light. It was as if all energy flowed away from her.

"Eliza, look at me!" She could feel Lucas tug at her shoulders to face him.

She met his gentle gaze, and her breath caught at seeing so much love and care in the boy's eyes. Without a thought, she fell into his open arms. They closed around her, and he pressed her closer. The book hung loosely from her hand as she let herself cry on his shoulder. That man, that awful, awful man had taken the life of one of her friends, the husband to one of the women who cared for her, and for what, for money? To make a business deal easier? The world of adults had always been confusing to her, but this made no sense at all. As her tears ran out, anger took sadness's place, and she could feel her resolve grow. Gently, she pushed away from the boy, drying her eyes with the back of her sleeved arm. She would have time to mourn her friend later, but first, his killer would come to justice.

Lucas, with the journal tucked under his arm, followed Eliza back to the locked door. She placed the key in the lock, and with closed eyes and crossed fingers, she tried to turn it. It wouldn't turn. Eliza tried again, putting more force into it, but it changed nothing.

The door remained locked. She was about to curse at the door when the sound of footsteps echoed down the hall. The children turned to each other, fear eminent on their faces.

As quickly and as silently as they could, they ran back towards the open room behind them and hid on each side of the door. Lucas clamped a hand over his mouth, trying to stop the sound of his heavy breathing. The footsteps grew closer until they stopped right outside the room. Eliza could hear a set of keys jingling and a lock turning. Lucas met Eliza's eyes as the figure outside moved in to the room, he then laid the journal down on the floor. It was then that Lucas did something Eliza hadn't expected him to do. He moved out of the room, and disappeared. She whispered his name, but too afraid to be spotted, stood still in her hiding spot.

Why is it always he who takes these risks? She thought to herself with a silent huff. Gently, and without making a sound, Eliza moved to see out the open door.

As quiet as a mouse sneaking it's way past a cat, Lucas edged his way closer to the now open office. He tried to hear what the person inside was doing, but it was difficult over the sound of the music from downstairs. Quickly, he poked his head into the door. The assistant of Mr Malfort, the mouse man, stood by a large wooden desk, raffling through paper and muttering to himself. His eyes were firmly on the papers before him and he hadn't seen Lucas. The man sighed, ran a hand through his hair, and turned around, walking towards a bookcase on the other side of the room. Lucas ducked his head as the man moved. This would possibly be the only chance they would have to get the papers. He crouched down low and moved.

Eliza wanted to run up and drag Lucas back from the open door, but she knew that they would be spotted, and she stayed rooted to the spot. Her eyes flittered to the boy, to the end of the hall, then to the open door. If they got out of this alive, she would give him a swift kick to the shin for his stupid ideas. After giving him the biggest hug. She watched as he disappeared through the door, her lip caught between her teeth and her hands shaking.

Never taking his eyes away from the man, Lucas crawled towards the desk. The man was rummaging through some books, clearly looking for something, and not finding it. Lucas could feel his frustration rolling off him in waves. It couldn't be the easiest job in the world, he thought to himself. Keeping his eyes on the man, Lucas nearly bumped his head on the desk as he reached it. Slowly, he crept around it, planning to hide himself under the desk until the man had gone. A noise from the hall made both stop in their tracks and look towards the door. With a nervous swallow, so loud that Lucas could hear it, the man walked briskly out of the room.

The boy let out a breath. Slowly, he raised himself up, keeping most of his body hidden, but high enough to see through the papers on top of the desk. He had no idea how long the assistant would stay away, or if it had been Eliza that made the noise.

Minutes passed as he search, sweat running down his temples as his heart raced. Finding nothing, Lucas started to open the drawers beside him. His shoulders drew up as his movements became frantic. Just as he hit bottom on the final drawer, he found a leather bound book. He picked it up, shaking it so to see if any loose papers would fly out. Nothing fell out. Flipping through it, reading the few lines in between, he came upon a page where a piece of paper had been attached to the original page. Gently, as not to rip it, Lucas took it apart, and unfurled it. In his hands lay exactly what they were looking for. The deed to the house. A smile grew on his face and his heart soared. Running out of the room, he had forgotten about the arrival of the assistant, his mind only on Eliza.

The girl stood huddled by the door, eyes wide as she saw him coming towards her. His smile brought hope into her, and her eyes caught the piece of paper he held. Eliza had picked up the journal and was ready to go as soon as Lucas was close enough. Only then did a thought occur to her, how would they be able to climb down with the book in hand?

"I got it! I found the paper!" Lucas all but yelled in his glee.

"That's wonderful, I'm so proud of you!" The boy preened under the praise but took a step back at the murderous glare Eliza then sent him.

"Just don't do anything as reckless as that again!" He could only nod at her harsh words.

Eliza voiced her concerns then, asking him what he thought about their escape. Should they try climbing down the way they came in, or should they find a new exit? Lucas thought about it, his brows furrowing and his free hand ran through his hair.

"What if… what if we sneak our way out the main door? Most of the guests are in the ballroom, and we have sneaked our way around worse places then this?" Eliza wanted to bring up how well that had gone the last time, but it didn't do to start arguing now.

Her unease with heights and the weight of the book would make it near impossible to get out that way. She saw no other alternatives at that point. Adrenaline and worry surged within the two children. They were not out of danger yet. If they were caught, the entire evening would have been for nothing, and neither knew what would happen to them then. With a quick nod, Eliza signalled for Lucas to follow her.

As they moved down the hall, she tried to picture the main entrance from where they were then, and were they had climbed in. The house was formed like a large brick, so the door must be sat at the other end of them, in the middle. Hopefully, they would just have to climb down the stairs, walk across a hallway and into the main hall. Without being spotted. Easily enough, Eliza hoped. She took the deed from Lucas' hands, placing it in the pages of the journal. That way, she hoped, it wouldn't get lost when they ran.

Music poured towards them as they started their descent of the stairs. It was large and dark, with a carpet running from top to bottom, muffling their steps. Even through the music, Eliza could hear her heartbeat, its pounding clear in her ears. Voices coming from around the corner at the end of the stairs made them stop. The voices moved away after a few minutes, and the children started down again. They reached the landing and started towards where they hoped the main hall would be.

The large house seemed to breathe around them. Tapestries, portraits and heavy curtains obscured the dark red walls. The end of the hallway came into view, and that's when they saw it. The main door. No guards, footmen or servants could be seen. The children shared a look. They would make it! The door was right there, and then they would be safe. They were just a couple of steps away from the door, Eliza had even reached out her hand, aiming for the doorknob, when a shout stopped them dead in their tracks. Their heads shot to the side where the assistant of Mr Malfort stood, coming out of a door on their left. Lucas gave a yelp, and Eliza gasped. The man, looking more bedraggled then any of them had seen him, looked between the children, down to the book in Eliza's arms, then to the door. The surprise on his face morphed into fear, and he took a shaking step towards them. In response, they took a step back, to the right. For a few moments, no one moved. Then, as if snapped out of a dream, Lucas took Eliza's free hand, and they ran, leaving the main door behind them.

***

The ballroom was decked out in the finest drapery, gold and decorations for the occasion. The massive chandelier had been polished, the floor shined, and the orchestra played as if for a king. Mr Malfort took great care in his gatherings and balls, it was one of the things he prided himself on. Usually, he arranged it so that the guests where a mixture of wealthy business folk and people who endeavoured to be in his favour. This night was no exception. He stood to the side, a glass of wine in hand, watching his guests mingle, dance and gossip. His eyes honed in on one woman in particular. Mrs Victoria Hardbrook had accepted his invitation, and with luck on his side which it usually was he would be able to make her accept his offer. Of course, the deed was already in his hands, but not legally. He could not start the building or gather the right people without causing suspicion. The investors had no idea he had not gotten her permission to buy the estate, and the longer it took for her to agree, the more likely the chance of them losing interest and demanding their money back became. His brows drew together as he watched her talking with the woman she came there with. He would hate to have to get rid of them, they were such beautiful creatures, and Mr Malfort had always had a weakness for pretty things. By the end of the night, he would have his way. One way or the other, the deal would *not* fall through. A smile tugged at the corners of his lips. He always got his way.

With a bang, the door to the great room flew open, and two faces he had made sure he would never see again stood at the entrance. With a *clink* the crushed wine glass in his hands fell to the floor in pieces. The children look shocked and afraid, eyes roaming the great hall as if searching for someone. His assistant then came running in after them, grabbing both by the shoulders. A murmur ran through the room, and the musicians stopped playing.

"Ladies, Gentlemen, no need to fret!" His voice rose to be heard over the crowd. "Seems my assistant has caught two beggar orphans looting my house!" He stepped closer to the children as he spoke. "I will deal with this, go back to your enjoyments. Music, if you please, dear orchestra!" His eyes zeroed in on Eliza.

The boy wriggled, trying to get free. The girl, however, stood still, eyes never stopping her search of the room.

"Victoria! Anne! Help!" She called out, voice cracking, as if she was fighting back tears. His assistant shushed her, pulling on her shoulder before looking up fearfully at his employer.

Two figures emerged from the chaos of people, stopping right within sight of both children and the master of the house.

"What is the meaning of this? Let go of those children this instance!" Victoria's voice was strong and cold as she spoke.

"As you can see, dear Mrs Hardbrook, these children are trespassing on my property, and as such, I can remove them if I so please." Mr Malfort answered. He gave her a fake smile and a little laugh directed at the rest of the room.

"No, let us go!" Eliza screamed, fear and desperation evident in her voice. "Vict-Victoria! I have it, I have what we came for!" At this, Mr Malfort shot the child a questioning look.

He walked quickly over to the girl, grabbing her arm that held the book, hard enough to bruise, and raised it to his face. He at once noticed the piece of paper sticking out of it, and with one quick movement, snapped it out. His eyes widened at the revelation and sweat started to form on his hands. He hadn't even hear Victoria starting to speak until she mentioned the deed.

"So, as you all see, this man is a fraud, a thief and a kidnapper!" Filled with anger, Victoria's voice was heard reverberating around the great room.

Murmurs started up again. People exchanged looks, and someone even shouted out about contacting the police. Ice ran through Mr Malfort, his heart threatening to break out of his chest. He smiled, trying to appear unfazed by the accusations. He would not go down without a fight.

"You mean to tell me you would believe a street urchin on some false account, over me? The man most of you have known for years?" Although he said it with confidence, Mr Malfort's eyes flittered between the inhabitants of the room, hands shaking. The hand that held Eliza's arm tightened.

Victoria took one step towards the man, holding the piece of paper in one hand, eyes narrowing as she spoke.

"I have all the evidence I need, *and* these people know me, as well. I believe these children. There is no use in trying to lie your way out of this, Mr Malfort, I know the truth. Everyone in this room knows it too. You shake like a leaf, and your eyes betray you. Face up to what you have done and turn yourself in to the police!"

Mr Malfort knew that the woman knew of the deed. What he did not know, was her ignorance over who had had a finger in her husband's death. His mind shut down, leaving only one thought behind. Escape. Victoria was close enough to touch the girl, hand's reaching out to take her away from the man. In a blink of an eye, Mr Malfort shocked the room. No one knew he had it on him, no one knew he even owned one, so when Victoria saw the gun he had produced, shock took over. Someone screamed at the sight, another yelled out for people to run. A stampede proceeded, yet Victoria took no notice. Without thinking, she lunged herself forward and said something Eliza would remember for the rest of her life.

"No, not my child!"

The following bang made the entire house shake, or so it felt to Eliza as she hit the floor. Pain engulfed her entire body. Screams and footsteps were all she could hear. Her eyes watered, and darkness loomed around her. A small body appeared next to her, shaking her shoulders. Lucas, it could only be him. He pulled her up, making her stand before pulling her aside. Two men ran past them before they reached out and fell holding down a screaming Mr Malfort. The gun lay a few feet away from him. Anne, Eliza realised, lay next to a body a few steps away from her. Eliza could barely hear what was going on, everything felt so muffled, as if she was wearing headphones. Streaks of warm acid ran down her cheeks. She was crying. Lucas was pulling on her, trying to get her away from the struggling man on the floor. Eliza saw it out of the corner of her eyes, for they had not left the lump on the floor. Why was Victoria's gown lying there? Why was Anne sitting by it, hiding the rest of it from them? Why were there other people huddling around them? Finally, she broke free from Lucas' grasp, crawling away from him, and falling beside Anne.

Victoria's face looked unchanged. Most of her hair had fallen out of the updo and lay in a halo of gold around her. Her eyebrows were knitted together in pain and her lips were trembling. Eliza couldn't hear what

Anne was saying, only feeling her hands move up and down the side of Victoria's arm. Eliza could see the tears flowing from the other woman, and neither made no motion to hide it. Sorrow burrowed into Eliza's heart and coursed through her veins with every beat. She didn't need to see the wound to know what Victoria had done for her. Time seemed to freeze, and everything around them, disappeared.

Eliza was vaguely aware of Mr Malfort being removed from the hall. She barely felt Lucas leaning into her side. The only thing she could focus on was the trembling lines of Victoria's mouth, and the words she had uttered. Eliza, with all the sureness of a 12-year-old, knew she would be okay. Nothing bad could happen to the ones you love. Everyone knew that. They needed to get her home. Victoria needed to be at home with Anne, Lucas and her. Eliza said as much, even if she couldn't hear the words. She said it again when no one listened. She yelled it, or she thought she did, trying to get Anne to listen. Why wouldn't she listen? If the worst thing happened, Eliza didn't even want to think it, Victoria needed to be in the home. She had seen her, she had seen them all, that night in the attic. Victoria and Anne with Gerald. They had to get her home.

Lucas disappeared from her side, she hardly noticed, and it wasn't until he was back, tugging at her dress that she took her eye's away from the woman on the floor. Anne too met Lucas' gaze. Whatever he had said, made Anne smile. It was wavery, and didn't reach her eye's, but it was a smile. Two men came then and helped pick Victoria up. Eliza walked with her arms around Lucas. He had bent down and picked her up. Usually she would have fought him for even trying, but she had no energy left. Just as they made their way out of the main door, Eliza's eyes gave in and closed.

***

It had been raining for days. Eliza could see it from where she sat on the carpet in the living room. Victoria's cold hand clasped hard in her hand, and Lucas' head resting on her shoulder. They had made it home, that night, in a burrowed cart. They had laid Victoria down on the main couch in the living room and had all stayed there. Anne, Lucas and Eliza had taken turn sitting beside the woman, having the butler bring in tea and food every couple of hours. The doctor had been there, talking in hushed voices with Anne. It had been the only time the children had not been allowed to sit near Victoria. Eliza had screamed when Anne had ushered them out the door. Her hearing had not returned fully, and it had taken some time for Lucas to explain what the doctor had said. Eliza had refused to listen, not ready to believe they could do nothing but wait. That the only comfort they could give was to sit by her side, making sure she was never alone. Eliza had thrown herself onto Victoria's still body when she was allowed back inside.

Lucas had tried to pull her off and earned a slap to the face for his action. He held her close as she broke down.

Eliza had buried her head between her legs as she sat on the floor. The hand that held Victoria cramped at the awkward angle, but it was the last of her worries. Dragging her thumb along the woman's wrist, Eliza let out a startled cry. Anne, who had been sleeping on a chair beside the couch shot up at the sound. Lucas jumped away as Eliza stood, hovering over Victoria. Anne came up beside her, placing one hand below her dear friends jaw, before kneeling and shaking her head. Lucas moved to place a tentative hand on Anne's back. The woman turned and engulfed the boy in a hug, shuddering as sobs escaped her. Eliza stood still, shaking her head. No. No. No. Without thinking, Eliza moved. She walked backwards until she was close to the front door. She turned around, opened it, and ran.

Rain and wind was all Eliza could feel. She refused to feel anything else. The country side gave way to busy streets, and soon tall buildings and people filtered in and out of view. The skies had darkened as she walked, soon it would be night and freezing. She didn't care.

Victoria's gone. Victoria's gone and it is all my fault. Like a mantra, the though ran around in her head until it was all she could hear. She walked for minutes, or hours. So focused on nothing, she barely manage to jump out of the way of a speeding cart. Stumbling backwards, heart beating and anger burning in her chest, the dull notes of music floats through the air. At first,

Eliza doesn't think anything of it, but then it hit her, it's the first thing she's been able to hear clearly since the ball. Up to her right, and old gothic building, with columns and statues stood empty.

Why is the music coming from the empty building? Eliza wondered.

Slowly, she walked up towards the entrance. It's locked. Her feet moved as she walked around the entrance, looking over the building. Trying to see what was making the music, Eliza almost walked by the little opening. Between two planks, Eliza makes it inside. The music is still low, but guides her along the large, dark hall, up a flight of stairs, until she stands before a large set of doors. With a bang, they give way to her touch. Everything inside was dark, yet she was barely able to see the chairs and stairs leading down towards an empty stage. Golden statues and cobwebs line the walls along the heavy, dark curtains.

As Eliza stepped forward, she feels rather than hears the music grow. A single candle alight on the stage before her. A voice suddenly joins the music, and Eliza feels it beckoning her forwards, taking control of her body, making her move slowly closer. A face, pale as the moonlight appears, crowded by heavy black curls that float around it. Could it be a woman? Eliza wondered. The music grows and spreads around the room, filling it. She feels no fear, only a pull, a need to hear more and to see more. As the music grows louder, the figure a woman on the stage became clearer. Still opaque, still a ghost, Eliza is sure about that, but now more alive. Eliza felt sure that if she leaned in close enough, she could touch her. Big doe-like eyes find Eliza's, and in that moment, the room changes. A gust of wind filled the space yet doesn't diminish the music and brought colours to all it touched. Lights fill the room as the music reached crescendo and peaks, and applause roars throughout the hall. Eliza turned around, finding herself in a filled opera house, and a standing ovation that nearly drowns out the sweet voice of the angel-like figure on stage. She turned back around, eager to share in the joy and again she locked eyes with the woman on stage. She looked as alive as Eliza felt. The ghost breaks out in the warmest smile Eliza had ever seen someone give, bowing her head in thanks, when the spell breaks. The room floods with darkness, and then she is alone again, gasping for breath. The music continued beating inside her chest with a melody Eliza would never forget.

Chapter 16
To Remember

A year had passed. Eliza couldn't imagine how the time had flown. With a shiver, she tugged the shawl closer around her shoulders. Her new dress, a birthday present from Anne, trailed behind her on the frozen ground. She had been old enough to start wearing a full length gown, the woman had told her. A few loose curls dangled in front of her eyes, they had escaped from the updo Anne had shown her how to do. She still had trouble making it look right on her own. After the funeral of Victoria, Anne had given her a present, something Victoria had asked her to give to the girl, in case of her passing. Victoria's ring, dangling from a thin golden chain, hung loosely around Eliza's neck. It's small weight letting her know that she would always have a piece of the woman with her. It was also, after the funeral, when Anne had asked both children to stay with her. The house, left to her by Victoria, was too large to live in alone, and there was no one else she would rather spend her life with, than the two children.

A few weeks later, when everything had calmed down, Anne, Eliza and Lucas had gone into town to have a family picture taken. Lucas had been nervous, saying it would be his first time, but Eliza had comforted him, promising to hold his hand throughout the picture. The finished picture hung on the wall above the fireplace, showing the family in their Sunday best, standing close together, and with serene looks on their faces.

The road ahead of her showed signs of winter already, even if November had just started. With quick steps, Eliza moved towards the house. Anne had sent her into town to pick up some more vegetables for supper, and she had gladly gone, it gave her a chance to run by the book store. Her little allowance, saved from three months ago and up until that day, had given her the opportunity to purchase a new book she had had her eyes on. At times like that, Eliza missed the collection of books from her own time. Her heart clenched painfully, as it always did when she thought of her past; the family she had left behind, and the life that was going on without her. Yet, even as the thought whirled around in her head, Eliza refused to listen. What good would thinking about it do? She had made her peace with the life she had.

It had been months since she last tried to locate the portal, without luck. After a while, she had simply given up hope of ever returning. With a deep sigh, she shook her head and fixed her gaze on the familiar house at the end of the street. This was her home. The people who lived there were her family. She pictured Anne, sitting by the fireplace, knitting Lucas another pair of mittens. His hands still grew, and with all the work he did, they wore out quickly. Smiling to herself, she thought about Lucas, her sweet friend, her brother in this life. He had quickly offered to do anything he could to help around the house, saying how he would like to work for his food and keep. Anne had shut that thought down quickly, letting him know that he was part of the family now, and that he no longer needed to worry about his next meal, or a safe place to sleep. That night, they had all sat on the large couch in the living room, holding each other close. The pain of losing Victoria had drawn them closer together, and they made it clear to anyone who asked them, that they were a family.

Hearing the sound of wood splintering, Eliza smiled to herself. Even if Anne had told him he had no need to work for her, he still found work that needed to be done around the house. Eliza often found him in the garden, turning the soil, or helping Anne put up a greenhouse for her plants. As Eliza turned the corner of the house, leading into the garden, she could see him standing with his back to her, chopping wood. He was her best friend, and the thought of living out her life there, seemed more bearable with him next to her.

"Hello, Lucas, hard at work?" He jumped at her words, axe falling from his hands and almost landing on his foot.

"Oh, you gave me a fright, Liza! Can't sneak up on a man like that." After his 15th birthday, Lucas had taken to calling himself the man of the house. Eliza and Anne usually shared a look whenever he said it but humoured him enough not to comment on it.

She laughed at him, mumbling an apology, before walking into the house. Eliza could hear Anne softly singing from the kitchen. The sound spread a warmth within her and she followed the sound. Anne stood by the kitchen table, washing some apples while she sang.

"Oh, good, you've returned!" Anne said as she caught sight of the girl.

"Wonderful, wonderful. And did you get to buy your new book?" The woman took the basket of vegetables from Eliza as she spoke. Her hands picking up item after item, examining it, before placing them down on the table.

"Yes, I did, thank you. Do you need anything, or can I help with anything, or may I go and start reading before supper?" Eliza asked.

"No, thank you my dear, I don't think I- Oh, wait! It might be a long shot, but I would love some mushrooms, and I see you didn't buy any." Eliza hung her head as the woman spoke, silently cursing herself for her foolishness in forgetting.

"Would you be a dear girl and see if you can find any more in the woods? I picked a bunch just last week, near the house. You won't have to go far," Anne continued.

Eliza nodded, pulled her shawl around her shoulders she moved towards the garden again. She picked up another, smaller basket before opening the door. As she passed Lucas, she called out to him.

"Just going to look for mushrooms, be back in a tiff!" She was close to the woods as he answered.

"All right, be safe, Liza, and don't take too long, I'm starving!" She waved him off with a laugh. That boy was always hungry.

Humming to herself as she walked, Eliza let her mind run empty. The sounds of the forest settling in for winter made her feel calm. It was when she could no longer see the house through the trees when the snap of a twig startled her. Out of the bushes, a little to her right, jumped a little rabbit. Her eyes went big as she looked at it, a memory slowly trickling back. Afraid of the rabbit getting hurt or eaten by foxes, Eliza made to pick it up. As if sensing her move, the rabbit jump out of reach, and set off, into the woods. Cursing to herself, Eliza set off after it. The basket and the shawl fell to the ground, forgotten.

Over patches of mud and frozen ground, she ran; jumping, moving and stumbling her way through the overgrown woods. Eliza struggled to keep the rabbit within sight. She ran until the air in her lungs felt like acid fog, and her eyes watered from the cold sting of the wind. Not looking down, Eliza missed the root jutting out from the ground, only realising its existence as she fell towards the ground, having stumbled over it. She rolled, in what must have looked like an awkward somersault out of the crowded forest and into a clearing.

With pain aching its way up her arm, Eliza tried to stand up. It was then that she saw it. A few feet before her, sat the rabbit. Its eyes were fixed in her, but behind it was something Eliza had not seen for a long time.

It was barely visible. The moss covered rock looked the same, but the small patch of shimmering light floated in the air. Had it not been for the slight sunshine filtering through it, Eliza wouldn't have even noticed its existence. She looked from the portal, down to the rabbit, and then back up. It was as if the universe was testing her, she thought. When she had finally come to terms with her new life, the old one showed itself once more. Something bubbled up inside of her and tears brimmed in her eyes. No, she wanted to shout. No, no, no! She wanted to stay, she *had* to stay, for Lucas, for Anne. No. She would pick up the now still rabbit and walk away. She had made her choice. So, when the rabbit made to jump away again, Eliza shot forwards, trying to catch it before it disappeared again. Tripping over her own legs, Eliza could only feel the weight and fluff of the rabbit in her arms as she fell once more. More bruises would appear, she thought to herself.

The rabbit wriggled in her hold as she stood up, dragging her free hand down her dress in hopes of removing the dried leaves and dirt from it. She sighed as she lifted the bunny towards her face to give it a stern glare.

"That was not very nice!" Eliza said.

Now, she had to find her way back to the house. It was all vaguely familiar to her, and she was positive she was going in the right direction. The sun shone weakly through the November skies, giving her a bit more warmth that the lost shawl would have provided. As she walked, Eliza felt herself tripping more over her dress than the sticks and terrain of the woods. Her shoes, the pair Anne had lent her, felt too large on her feet. Annoyance grew within her as twigs pulled at her hair and scraped along her arms. Suddenly, she could hear shouting from up ahead. Her name was being yelled. She hadn't been gone *that* long, and she saw no reason for Lucas to be yelling for her.

"Yes, yes, I'm coming! Don't get riled up, Lucas, I'm almost there!" Even her voice sounded angry to herself, even if she didn't mean it.

The voices grew, however, and they sounded less and less familiar. Eliza stopped walking, her eyebrows furrowing and her breathing heavy. Nothing about the yelling sounded right. Nothing, in that moment, *felt right*. With shaky steps, Eliza started to walk again, getting closer and closer to what she now realised must be the path to the house. Quicker and quicker, until she was running. There, she could see it, the house. But who was that standing in front of it? That wasn't Lucas? That was… that was her father, and he was calling for her.

"Eliza! Eliza where have you been? I've been waiting for ever. You knew I was coming to pick you up today, right?" It was her father, standing in front of the house she had called home for over a year. Yet, it wasn't the same, not really.

Eliza felt as if a frozen stone had been shoved down her throat, that she was not in her time any more. She stopped her walking, limbs unwilling to move as much as an inch as the terror of her reality sunk in. Tears flowed down her cheeks, and her head shook, as if willing the realty to change if she believed in it enough.

This isn't real. This isn't real! It became too much. Eliza could feel her body shutting down, yet she couldn't feel the coldness of the ground as it welcomed her.

The sound of a car's engine starting up wrestled her out of her sleep. She could feel the cool glass pressing against her face where she sat in the back seat. With a broken sob, Eliza fixed her gaze up at the old house, eyes straining to see the top windows. Just as the car started to drive away, three familiar faces looked down and met her gaze. New tears flowed freely as Eliza lifted her hand and waved goodbye to the people who had meant so much to her, who had become her family; who would always have a place in her heart. Her eyes drifted from Gerald, to Victoria, and finally, to Anne. Their own smiles were sorrow filled, and Eliza knew that if they could, they too would be crying. Yet, she knew, it wasn't a farewell. She would see them again. As the car sped up, and the sights outside blurred, Eliza took out the necklace she had hidden under her dress. Victoria's ring felt familiar in her hands and gave her comfort in those moments before her eyes, again, grew heavy, and darkness welcomed her back, like an old friend.

Epilogue

The graveyard was empty. Not unusual, during the early afternoon. A slow trickle of rain drummed on the stones, grass and on the bench Eliza sat on. The umbrella she had brought perched crookedly against her shoulder. In her lap lay letters and a few photographs. Her fingers grazed each page of the letter she was currently reading, a smile dancing on her lips. Time had moved slowly in her own time. Catching up to the one year anniversary of her returning hadn't been easy or fast. For the first few weeks, on every weekend, she had begged to go back to her grandparents' house. Tears of sorrow and anger at her parents refusal, week after week, had worn them down until the day she was allowed to go back. Her clothes had been easy to lie about, she had just explained that she had found them in a small shed in the woods. They had believed her, thinking the clothes to be part of a costume. The rabbit, on the other hand, had not. Eliza's father had quickly deposited the animal down on the ground when she had stepped out of the car and he had to physically restrain the girl from going after it, calmly stating that under no circumstances would that wild thing be allowed into their home. Eliza had refused to talk to him for three days.

Once back at her grandparents' house, Eliza had wasted no time in running back into the woods. Three hours later, she had come wandering back, eyes red and puffy, with shoulders slumped and no words to give her worried grandparents. Just before midnight, Eliza had snuck back up to the attic. To her great sorrow and slight surprise, no one came to her that night. She had sat in the attic for over five hours, alone, willing her friends to appear. After breakfast, she had again run back to the woods. With no rabbit, and no portal in sight, Eliza had taken to wandering around the surrounding area. It was then that she had found the shed. It looked the same, run down and overgrown, and it lit up hope within the girl.

It was the same as it had been the last time on the inside as well. Broken pottery, dust and dead leaves littered the ground. Eliza made a beeline for the shelf where she had first found photographs of her friends. The box was still there, and she opened it with fervent hands. The first picture she had found lay waiting for her. Tears broke free at the sight. with gentle fingers, Eliza picked it up and studied it for a minute. With a featherlight kiss to the photo, she placed it on the shelf. Picking up the letters, Eliza could see the signature of both Anne and Victoria on them. She flipped through a few until an unopened letter caught her attention. It was addressed to her. Eliza drew in a sharp breath, nearly dropping the box in her shock. Careful not to rip the delicate paper apart, she opened it. In nearly faded ink, Eliza was able to read.

October. 1891.

Dearest Eliza. It has now been a year since your parting. We, Lucas and I, do hope it was home that you went to. Anything else is not something I want to put on this page. I, well, we, hope you find this letter one day, and hope it finds you well. Lucas wants me to write that he is not mad at you, and that he misses you with all his heart; as do I, dearest one. I also wish to say that we are well. Do not fret for us, dearest. I shall take good care of Lucas, and in time, he shall take good care of me. He was insistent in wanting to leave you a letter himself, and it should be with the other letters, where you located this.

Remember to live in the now, dearest. It does not do to dwell on the past. Life is meant to be lived going forwards, not looking back. I love you with all my heart, my dearest child. Until we meet again.

Anne.

Eliza had to place her head on her own shoulder to keep her tears from hitting the letter. Broken sobs shook her frame and she clutched the letter to her heart. Once she returned to her grandparents' house, she made straight for her room. The overnight bag she had brought emptied quickly as she tossed every item of clothing out to make room for the small box. It would stay with her, and no one was to take it away from her. Her parents had even tried to take Victoria's ring away, afraid that the girl had stolen it from her grandmother. At the screams of fury and pleading, they had let her keep it. Eliza had refused to take it off. Emotionally drained, she had fallen into bed, and sleep had once more claimed her.

***

Lucas's letter lay at the front of the pile on her lap. The rain fell heavier, coating the bottom of her shoes where they dangled. It had taken Eliza quite some time to find his grave. Hours at the local library looking up Lucas Richards (for he had taken Anne's name), and his place of burial. It was after months of research that she had found it, and more. It had come as quite the shock when she found out that her grandmother's maiden name was Richards. A part of her was both overjoyed, and a little sad, by the fact that her closest friend was her own great-great grandfather. It would explain why the house had stayed in her family. He had taken care, telling his children to be sure to either keep the house in the family, or only sell it to those they trusted. It seemed a little crazy, how could it be? He couldn't have possibly known. She hadn't even known.

Eliza took up the boy's letter, having lost count of how many times she had read it. It still made her smile, and her heart would tug painfully at his carefully drafted words. He had meant the world to her and would stay with her no matter what.

January 1892.

To Eliza.

Oh, Eliza, what should I write to you? I miss you more than I have words to describe. But you already know that. We are doing all right, Ms Anne is helping me with my reading and writing and has promised to one day help me find a reputable job. She's also promised to keep me safe. A part of me doesn't believe my luck, but I'm far from the idiot who asks why the goose lays golden eggs. I think I'll be fine, despite you not being here to look after me. I promise not to get into any mischief, though if we're being honest, you were the one who got me into it. Remember that we are your family, and if we're thinking about you, you ain't alone.

Your brother, now and forever.

Lucas. R.

Inside the envelope lay a faded old photo, one Eliza recognised immediately. The kind faces of Anne and Lucas stared back up at her. Her eyes looked back with a contentment she hadn't felt in such a long time. Carefully, she laid everything back into their new envelope, making sure they were all secure from the rain and dirt, before placing them back into her backpack.

The graveyard was empty, in one way. There was no living person besides the young girl on the bench. Eliza could see four or five spirits going about their business among the gravestones and shrubberies. The gift had not gone away or held itself to her grandparents' house. They did not scare her, nor did they interact with her. Most of them didn't even acknowledge her being there. Eliza was okay with that. She was there to mourn, and to reminisce, not to chat. With a sigh, her eyes fell back to the grave in front of her. She raised the letters, the dates and the name one more time. Then she stood up, pulled the small bouquet of flowers from her bag and placed them on the overgrown grass. With a final look, Eliza placed a hand atop the grave, dragging her thumb over it, as she had once done with his hands.

"Goodbye, brother. Until we meet again."

The End.